Letters to Saint Lydia

a novel by
Melinda Johnson

CONCILIAR
PRESS

Chesterton, Indiana

Letters to Saint Lydia

Published by   Conciliar Press
                   A division of Conciliar Media Ministries
                   P.O. Box 748
                   Chesterton, IN 46304

Printed in the United States of America

ISBN 10: 1-936270-08-0
ISBN 13: 978-1-936270-08-0

Cover photo by Stephanie A. Platis

15 14 13 12 11 10   6 5 4 3 2 1

For My Daughter
In all Life, there is a Trinity: a quest for the Father,
a birth of the Son, a breath of the Holy Spirit.

1

June 16

Dear Saint Lydia,

My name is Lydia. I was named for my agnostic grandmother, and I'm definitely not a saint. In fact, I'm not even a Christian, and I'd never heard of you until my family was baptized into the Orthodox Christian Church without me a few weeks ago. When we came home from the church, my mother followed me into my room and handed me a five-by-eleven icon of you. She made a point of explaining that an icon is more than just a picture, and she urged me to consider this gift as some kind of link to the real you. Although the anxious-hopeful look that came with the gift made me want to crawl out of my skin, the icon itself is kind of intriguing. It's been sitting on my bureau since she gave it to me, and for some reason, I catch myself staring at it any time I'm in the room for more than a few minutes.

The icon shows you with a halo behind your head. You're wearing a red dress with a yellow overdress. You have a blue scarf wrapped around your head and shoulders, and another one in your hands. Maybe there's a story about this scarf in your hands. You seem to be holding it out to someone. How old is this image, I wonder? Did someone who knew you paint it originally? Is this what you really looked like, or have you been stylized and idealized away from your actual self? I always wonder that when I see old paintings because none of them look like the real people walking around on earth today.

My family got baptized without me because I'm 17 and I chose not to join them, but it's not because I'm hostile to the idea, necessarily. It just doesn't make any sense, for many reasons. Being a saint, I'm sure you know all about Christianity, Orthodox and otherwise, but the only people I know who are Orthodox are Greek or Russian. My family is neither. And that's only the smallest reason why I find this whole situation bizarre.

So, are you real? Is that why I keep staring at you?

My anxious-hopeful mother says you are alive in heaven and can pray for me. I'm sure I need it, but I won't be asking you for prayers unless I decide to buy into the whole package—saints, prayers, real God to pray to in the first place. But I think there's no harm in writing to you. I can't resist, actually. I need someone to talk to.

It's dinner time. Now that my parents have got religion, we're all eating our evening meals together. It's friendly, I guess. Or it would be if I weren't the One Person Who Unfortunately Wasn't Baptized.

Sincerely,

Lydia

P.S. It looks so strange to see the same name at the start of the letter and the end of the letter. It's like I'm writing to myself. Maybe I am. I don't even know if you exist.

Dear Lydia,

I exist. And like you, I did not begin life as a saint! You are wise not to ask for my prayers until you believe I am real, but I will pray for you in the meantime because although you do not know me, I know you.

We have a problem in common, you and I. You do not know I am reading your letter, and so you are not reading mine. But like you, I will write just the same.

> May He hold you in the palm of His hand.
> Saint Lydia

2

June 17

Dear Saint Lydia,

I just read the first page of this journal, and I realized that if you're actually reading this, you must be wondering a lot of things now. But first, do you know who I am? Can you see me, or my family? Maybe you're looking down from heaven at millions of people on earth and wondering which ones we are. How much can saints see from up there? Are you like God? No, probably not. You were just a person in real life, even if you are holy now.

Let me introduce us, just in case. I can't tell my story unless you know the characters the way I know them.

My dad's name is Ned, and he's about 6 feet tall with dark brown hair and a pink face. I love my dad, but I wish he was more forceful about things. It's not that he doesn't stand up for himself about big issues, but it seems like he's always giving in on little issues. I don't give in on anything. If you let people decide the little things for you, they'll try to take over the big things, too. My mom's name is Nora, and she's blond and pretty and *vivacious* (I think this word was *invented* for my mother), but she doesn't give in on anything either. So there's Dad, who would rather make peace than make a point, and there's Mom and me, who are always battling over which of us is actually in charge of *me*. I wonder sometimes if she remembers how old I am. I doubt it.

Tirsa is my little sister. She's six years old. You'll never guess where she got her name. When my mom was pregnant with my sister, my parents were watching the movie *Ben Hur*, which is a movie from the 1950s about a chariot race between an ancient Roman and an ancient Christian, and there was a character named Tirsa. I don't know if my parents only liked her name or if they liked the character too, or maybe they were just feeling happy the day they watched it, but anyway, that's where Tirsa got her name.

I never thought much about Tirsa's name before, but explaining it to you suddenly made me question my explanation. I've heard this story many times and accepted it, but now it seems bizarre. Who names their baby after a fictional character? And what's even weirder, now that I think about it, is that the Tirsa in the movie was a Christian, and my parents definitely were not. Or so I thought!

Once they decided to be baptized, my parents told me that they wanted Tirsa to grow up "in the faith," but that at my age, it wouldn't mean anything for me to convert unless I believed in what I was doing. This surprised me a little, coming from them, but it's true. Full immersion and holy oil wouldn't make me any different if I didn't believe in them, would they?

Later,

Lydia

Dear Lydia,

I know who you are. You are right that I am "just a person," and not a god, but one can know more as a person here with God than is possible for human beings still in the world. When I look at you and think of you, the Holy Spirit speaks to me about your life and tells me what you need and what you love and what you try to accomplish. It is a different kind of knowledge, perhaps, than what you mean.

I am glad to know more of you from your own account and to learn about your family. At your time in life, the innocent trust you had in your parents as a child is waning, and it is difficult to feel at peace with them as you discover all their flaws. When you cannot talk to them, you can always talk to God. And you can talk to Mary, His mother, and to me, as you are doing.

Tirsa's name interests me. It suggests that your parents' reflections on their spiritual life began much earlier than you were aware. It is possible that they simply liked the name. But in light of their decision to convert to Orthodoxy six years later, their decision to name their child after a Christian woman (no matter how fictional) seems meaningful.

When you say that baptism would not change you if you did not believe in it, you are partly right. But one should never underestimate the inherent power of holy things. They have their own life, and they do not depend on your belief in them to make them real. Look at me! I existed before you ever spoke to me, and I exist now, when every moment you are asking yourself why you are so foolish as to write to me though you believe me to be long dead.

Perhaps you are writing to me because God has opened the door to your spirit a little way and you are just curious enough to wish to peek through the crack and see what is in that newly opened room.

In Christ,

Saint Lydia

3

Dear Saint Lydia,

Where was I?

Oh, yes. The family. Ned, Nora, Tirsa, and me, Lydia. I'm about average height, and my hair is like my dad's, dark brown, and so are my eyes, but my skin freckles in the sun. My face is kind of square, and so is my chin. I don't wear a lot of makeup because it takes too much time in the morning. When I was in eighth grade, my friends taught me how to put on makeup. Mom wears it, but not the way people my age do.

I graduated from high school right after my family was baptized, and in about two months, I'll be going away to college. I can't wait! Maybe I'm a tiny bit nervous. It's a big change to move away from home, but I really want to go. I'm tired of all the tension with my mom. I'm ready to try being out on my own. Right now, I'm still home, for the summer, with plenty of time to think deep thoughts and write them to a person who died 2000 years ago.

I'm proud to say I landed a summer photography internship at our town's newspaper, so I work there three or four days each week. Sometimes they stick me with all the boring administrivia, but a couple of the photographers are friendly; they let me tag along with them on assignments and try my hand at photo-editing and layout when the opportunity presents. The fact is, I'm slightly obsessed with photojournalism, and I'm crossing all my available fingers that I'll make it onto the yearbook staff when I get to college. I'm not sure they let lowly freshmen do anything that cool, but I'm sure going to try!

I don't know if you had reporters in your day, but in case you did, let me tell you that photographers are different from other journalists, in my humble opinion. We're behind the camera, not in front of it, so don't get the impression that I'm racing around with a big toothy smile, prying vital information out of helpless bystanders.

I'm actually a quiet person. I'm not shy exactly, but I'm inclined to think more than I talk until I warm up to people. I don't have a huge dating life, but I could probably go out more than I do if I would take the trouble. Girls who talk about nothing but boys annoy me. I read a lot, for fun, but I don't talk about it much. My books are my private world. I don't often feel the urge to invite someone into it. I consider myself a feminist, but I'm not insane about it. I'm a mediocre vegetarian, because I think it's healthy, but I do adore ham. My sport is volleyball, so I wish I were taller, but I have strong legs and a mean spike, so I can hold my own. My favorite colors are red and blue (go team!). What else? My favorite things are the feeling of new socks in new running shoes, the smell of butter melting on pancakes, and the way good books draw you so far in you don't even notice time passing. And I love rain. Especially rain in the summer that turns everything silver and green.

We have a dog named Rilla, which is short for Gorilla because she's big and black and furry, and she's a love monster. She wants to be hugged and patted and smothered with *love*. She's a woofing, snuffling, bouncing bundle of doggy joy. I love Rilla more than anything because Rilla loves me back, just plain, just because she does.

My best friends are Trella, Maria Louisa, Lauren, and Jill, and they were all on the volleyball team with me in high school. Trella is a super-star at everything, Maria Louisa is everybody's mama hen, Lauren is the constant talker, and Jill makes me laugh like a billy-goat. I love my whole team, actually, and I love them *as* a team, as a big group of girls all har-monizing with each other as players and as people. We've spent so much time together that we're always real with each other. It's like a family should be, only bigger. I'm going to miss them more than anything else about high school, but my little group of friends are all going to the state college to keep on playing volleyball, just like I am, which is a very, very good thing. I'll have ready-made friends there, instead of starting out a complete stranger to everybody.

I can't think of anything else to say right now. I wonder if you are reading this. How would I know?

Best wishes,

Lydia

Dear Lydia,

I am reading every word you write to me. Your letters bring me great delight.

Your mother seems to trouble you, dear girl. There is some constraint between you, something that makes you respond to her with frustration instead of trust. I do not know which of you is the source of the problem. You said earlier that neither you nor your mother ever "gives in," so it seems likely that this is a case of mutual stubbornness leading to mutual irritation. If you remember that she likely wants what is best for you, perhaps you can learn to forgive her when she tries too hard to provide it for you.

I can see that Rilla is precious to you because her love is simple and pure. All love is a gift from God, the source of love. God is love itself. Whenever you encounter a good love, know that God is present there. Rilla is God's creation, and when Jesus Christ lifted up all creation in His glorious resurrection, He brought you this delight in your furry friend. It is a good gift.

I am glad to learn that you read a great deal. Your mind is precious, and the more you teach it, the better it will serve you. Reading is good for another reason, too. It stimulates the imagination, and I find that imagination is one way that human beings learn to believe in what they cannot see. What lives in the mind becomes so real that we begin to wonder if there may be other unseen things, other worlds not yet explored.

Do not worry when you have nothing to say. Some of the best moments in any friendship are those of companionable silence. Like your volleyball friends, I wish most of all to be "real" with you. I love your description of them, the many single souls willing to live and thrive for their common good. This is what God intends for us, the company of one another in the shelter of His love.

His blessing and His grace be upon you,
Saint Lydia

Dear Saint Lydia,

I need to explain to you why I'm not Orthodox. I know I already did explain it, but I feel compelled to explain more, in case you're actually reading what I write.

If what my mom says is true, you're Orthodox yourself, so you must be wondering why I don't get it.

This all makes me uncomfortable. Before my parents decided to convert, we weren't religious. I think I've been to church, any church of any kind, maybe ten times in my whole life, and those were all weddings or funerals, or Christmas Eve with Grandma. My parents always told us to be good, but they never told us why. That's what religion is, isn't it? It's *why* you should be good.

I don't understand why they turned religious. They said they felt a need in our lives, but I didn't feel a need in my life. We never even talked about religion in our family. How was I supposed to guess they wanted to? It's such a *new* thing for them to do. I don't even recognize my own parents, in a way.

Before all this happened, if people asked my parents what religion they were, they would always say that being out in nature was how they felt close to God and that we liked to go hiking to be in touch with our spirituality.

Frankly, that always sounded kind of silly to me. It sounded like one of those answers you make up and keep on hand to throw at anyone who bothers you. But what do I know? Maybe they really were thinking about God out there in the woods. Maybe they thought about God so much they made themselves curious.

The point is, I feel like I just landed on stage in the middle of a play, and I'm the only actor who doesn't know her lines. I don't even know what play this is. How did I get here? Why did my parents do this to us? Why do I have to be affected by it? How does it make anything better?

I tried going to one or two of their classes at church this past year, but the fact that we were there at all was so mentally confusing to me that I couldn't focus on what was being said. No matter how much great theology my mom offers me, I can't escape from my inner merry-go-round. I'm completely entangled in my own attempt to find some deeper reason for their decision. And the fact that I still live with them after deciding not to join them in this spiritual adventure makes life stressful and complicated. College can't come soon enough for me!

I'm not feeling what my parents want me to feel or thinking what they want me to think, so all I do is upset them or embarrass myself. They waited till three days before the baptism to tell me it was my choice whether I got baptized. It was painfully clear that they were hoping a miracle would happen and I would want to join them. To be honest, it seemed a little ridiculous to me when they told me it was my choice. I already knew it was my choice. Isn't it obvious that I'm too old to be told what to believe?

I'm not trying to be difficult, but seriously, they just changed our family completely, and it's going to take time for me to adjust to this. I did go to their baptism, and when my mom gave me the icon of you, I took it and said thank you, but now what do I do with it? What is she expecting me to do with it? Is she hoping your icon will convert me?

Everyone at their church was staring at me through the entire baptism service. There I was, standing over to the side, staring at the floor while my whole family became Orthodox without me. I felt like everyone was thinking, "What's wrong with her?" because I didn't become a Christian. But I just couldn't. It wouldn't mean anything except that I caved under pressure, and if there *is* a God (and I'm not saying there isn't), I don't think He would want me on those terms, would He?

Sincerely,

Lydia

P.S. If you weren't a saint and already dead, I would ask you not to tell anyone what I've said to you. When I try to express my views on this topic, it doesn't go well. I don't even talk to my friends about this. I tell them *everything*, but I don't know what I would say about this, and I don't want any more opinions on what I should do, thank you very much.

P.P.S. What I don't understand is, if my parents really think baptism will save my immortal soul, how come I get to choose whether I do it? Is it actually fine with everyone if I decide *not* to save my immortal soul?

Dear Lydia,

I am honored that you chose to confide in me, and I will certainly never break your trust.

I cannot write another word without telling you that God does want you!

Your instinct is correct that family pressure is no reason to become a Christian. But you must not then decide that God wants you only if you are baptized. He wanted you before you drew your first breath! He made you, Lydia. He knows how you feel even before you tell Him, and He understands your feelings better than you do yourself. He knows how unexpected and baffling this experience has been for you. Do not worry about God. He is right beside you, and He will still be there when you are ready to turn to Him.

I can see why you feel confused, and why you feel that you have been separated from your family. You did not expect this from your parents, you were not prepared for it, and it is so unfamiliar to you that you are not able to put it together with the many familiar things you know about your parents and your family life. What they are saying to you now is so different from anything they have said before that you cannot truly believe they mean it. You must be asking yourself how religion will fit into your personal world, the world of your family that never had room for religion before. How will a new set of beliefs change the old ways of making choices about life? Who are your parents and your sister, now that they are Orthodox?

I like your idea that religion is what explains "why you should be good." This is certainly true, although religion is much more than this. Most of all, religion is how we know God. In time, you may find that "religion" will clarify things in your family. It is always easier to interact with someone when you know the "why" behind their choices and actions. But it will take time to learn all the new reasons that come from this new faith, and it will also take time for you to feel at home with them, especially because you do not yet feel at home with the faith itself.

> *In prayer for you in your new home,*
> *Saint Lydia*

_5_

July 1

Dear Saint Lydia,

Now that you know about me, I decided I would find out about you.
I looked you up on Google and clicked a link to a Bible site that told your
story. The Bible is a place I don't go often, but I read enough to find out
who you are. This is what it said:

Acts 16:14–15 (New King James Version)
Now a certain woman named Lydia heard us. She was a seller
of purple from the city of Thyatira, who worshiped God. The
Lord opened her heart to heed the things spoken by Paul. [15] And
when she and her household were baptized, she begged us, saying, "If you have judged me to be faithful to the Lord, come to
my house and stay." So she persuaded us.

Is that it? What happened next? I wonder if it says more somewhere else.

I wonder who "Paul" was. I know a guy named Paul at school. I don't know him well. We seem to take the same classes, but we don't socialize outside of class very much. I think he keeps to himself. I would tell you about him except that it seems weird to be talking about boys with a saint.

I'm off to take Tirsa to the neighborhood swimming pool, her favorite destination. My friends Lauren and Jill are going to meet me there. We can lie in the deck chairs and talk till the sun goes down (or Tirsa gets tired). I love summer!

Au revoir,

Lydia

P.S. A seller of purple? What does that mean?

P.P.S. You and your household got baptized, but my household got baptized without me.

Dear Lydia,

You have found my story, or at least the part of it written down for you by Saint Paul. To say I was a "seller of purple" means that I sold cloth that had been dyed by a laborious process that made it a beautiful scarlet color (not the color you call "purple" today), and it was both expensive and highly prized.

I think you are relieved and sad that your household was baptized without you. It was different for me, Lydia. Do you see what Saint Paul says? The Lord opened my heart. There I was, standing on the riverbank, and my whole inner being shook, the way a bell trembles when it rings. Everything in me came to life. This is what you are looking for, that inner knowledge urging you to leap into the sacred water and stand up again reborn.

I knew what I heard from Saint Paul was true. When I rose up out of the water, I was filled with energy and joy. I invited Saint Paul and his companions to stay at my house because I was burning to give expression to all the love in my heart, to give back to them a little of the great gift they had shared with me. It was a way of celebrating what I felt inside and of cementing the promise of my baptism by action in my life.

Someday, when you can hear me, I will tell you the rest of the story.

I am interested to hear of this boy at school named Paul. It seems you think me a prudish, disapproving person. No doubt someone has been misinforming you about saints. You will be one yourself someday, Lydia, if you wish to be, and surely there would be nothing strange in "talking about boys" with you.

With a sigh,
Saint Lydia

6

July 1, Again

Dear Saint Lydia,

I know I said I was leaving for the pool, but I kept thinking after I stopped writing, so now I have to write again!

I will tell you one thing about Paul, and then you'll see why I'm not telling you anything else. I think Paul is what my mother would call a "bad boy." A bad boy, according to her, is a video-game junkie with a nose ring and tattoos who probably does drugs or sleeps around or, at the very least, blows off all his homework. I think there's more to it. I think a "bad boy" is a boy who does all that and is still good-looking. Full of charm. A babe magnet. A hottie. A stud muffin. In a word, attractive. Otherwise, who would care about him and his bad habits?

I doubt the Paul I know does drugs or anything, and he has short brown hair and wire-frame glasses, so he doesn't look like the nose-ring-tattoo type. He is unusually smart. But he's a smart mouth, too. He tries to make the teacher look stupid, and he shows his boredom when someone's doing a presentation. It's like the only voice he wants to hear is his own. There's a word for this. *Egomaniac.*

But if he was only an egomaniac and nothing else, there wouldn't be anything interesting about him. There's something about the way he does all these rude things that makes you wish he could get over the fact that he's smarter than most of the people around him. You can't help thinking, "Too bad. He could be so nice."

Maybe his problem is that he has no people smarts, only book smarts. Maybe he doesn't know how to talk to anything he can't put under a microscope. No one has ever seen him with a normal, mortal girl. But you never know. He's going to the state college too (because he got some big science scholarship there and his family can't afford anything else), so we'll probably see him around, dating some grad student prodigy who's specializing in astrophysics.

Look at me. Miss Don't Talk About Boys to a Saint has now written one, two, three, four paragraphs about a boy, *to a saint!*

I must be losing my grip.

Now I *am* going to the pool, so no more out of me today.

Lydia

Dear Lydia,

I see that although you have your moments of cynicism, you are learning to look upon your fellow human beings with an understanding eye.

It is truly a bitter thing to find a man who could be so much more than he is. If he is indeed in love with himself, he is closing himself to the world and turning inward, where he will suffocate and die.

We will hope for better things for this young man. Every child is born for heaven, even this "egomaniac," as you call him. Perhaps something has happened to him that grieves him or frustrates him. Perhaps his egotism is merely the face he shows to the world because he does not know how to do better. Perhaps he is only frightened. At some level, most people are. Most of the evil that comes into the world has its roots in the fear of death. It is a sickness, and only the knowledge of eternal life can cure it.

I will pray for this Paul, and of course I will pray for you, as I do always.

In Christ our Life,

Saint Lydia

7

July 1, Again!

Dear Saint Lydia,

I know I said I wouldn't write again today, but apparently you're becoming a habit!

Our afternoon at the pool was perfect. Tirsa and her little buddies kept themselves happy splashing around in the water, so Lauren and Jill and I lay on deck chairs and talked our heads off. We decided we looked like a box of crayons: Lauren is blond and had a yellow swimsuit on, Jill is a redhead and wore a red suit, and I was the brown crayon because of my très chic brown swimsuit and un-chic brown freckles.

Lauren thinks there's something going on with Trella (remember, the one who's a superstar at everything?). She keeps calling Trella to ask if she wants to go on a road trip to the beach, but Trella doesn't return her calls or says she's feeling sick and can't come. This is not like Trella at all. She's usually the most social person on earth and ready for anything. She's even friendly when you wake her out of a sound sleep at 5:00 AM to make an early game bus.

I thought Lauren should try again in a week or two when Trella might be feeling better (people do get sick, even Trella), but Jill has another theory. We all know that a couple months before graduation, Trella started dating a guy from another school. His name is Chad, and she met him sometime in the fall, at a party after a volleyball game. The rest of us never saw much of him, and we didn't see much of her either after she started dating him, but it was so close to the end of the year and graduation that nobody thought much about it.

Jill thinks Trella is having man trouble of some kind. Maybe they're fighting, or maybe they broke up. If we had gotten to know Chad well, like we usually do with each other's boyfriends, we'd be the first to know if they were fighting, and Trella would want it that way. But Chad never became part of our crowd, so maybe Trella feels awkward about discussing him with us. I didn't think anyone gave her grief for dropping us and spending all her time with Chad, but maybe someone did. Or maybe she thinks we will when she decides to come back to us.

Or maybe she really does have the flu! Trella is so *organized*. It's hard to imagine her involved in anything as messy as "man trouble."

Off to bed after I put some lotion on these freckles.

Lydia

Dear Lydia,

It occurs to me to wonder how well you and your friends truly know one another. You are happy in one another's company and mutually interested in one another's lives, but Trella's reluctance to confide in Lauren suggests that their friendship, at least, does not run deep. One might also question why Trella has not initiated a conversation with any of you three, if there is something troubling her. If her friendship with you is as strong as you all seem to feel it is, why are you left to guess at events as significant as a broken romance and, perhaps, a broken heart?

You are on the brink of a spiritual journey, dear girl, which you yourself will hesitate to speak of with these friends of yours. You have already failed to tell them that your family has converted to Orthodoxy without you, and yet this event is so significant to you that you are writing letters to an icon out of your deep need to talk to someone, even someone you have never met and do not wholly believe can hear you.

You are all young, and you are not yet expert in examining the nature of your relationships. You are too busy experiencing your lives to spend much time in studying their quality, but this is a skill you will need more and more as you enter fully into the complexities of mature adulthood. In a short time, the events of your own life and of Trella's will force you to begin this examination as you seek the friends who are coming with you on the journey and identify the friends who, by their own choice or by yours, will be left behind.

In Christ, who knows each one of us,
Saint Lydia

July 14

Dear Saint Lydia,

My mom wants to know if I want to go to church with them. What a loaded question that is. Do I "want" to? Why do people always use this word in a question to tell you what to do? A question should be for when it's really a choice, not for a confusing way to tell you what you're going to choose whether you like it or not.

No, I don't "want" to go. I'm sorry if that hurts your feelings. It's not about you personally. I'm sure church is great for some people. But what am I going to do there? They all know I wasn't baptized. It would just be embarrassing to go. Tirsa says they stand up for the whole service, and then they receive the body and blood of Christ, but she says I can't have it because I wasn't baptized.

Where to even start with that one . . . the body and blood? I know she's talking about communion, but why does she say it like that? Tirsa says it's not like I think. She says I would say it's like magic, in a way. Tirsa is so funny. She's like a little owl. She has brown hair, lighter than mine and soft like feathers, and she has a round little face with a perky little nose and round little glasses that make her eyes look big and round. She tilts her head a little to one side when she's thinking before she answers you, and then out comes the answer in her chirping little voice. A baby owl. Owls are supposed to be wise, of course, but Tirsa is smarter than you would expect from a six-year-old, so my simile still works.

Argh. Well, it's only Wednesday, so I still have some time to think. I'm off to go eat pasta and salad. No meat or cheese on Wednesday, because it's the day when Judas betrayed Jesus. That doesn't seem like a happy thing to be commemorating every single week. I wonder why they do that.

Of course, I could put cheese on *my* pasta, but when I tried doing it on the first Wednesday after they converted, all three of them watched me get the cheese, open the package, shake out the cheese, and eat it. Nobody said anything. They just looked. I haven't tried it since.

All for now,

Lydia

P.S. Tirsa asks what I'm doing in here, but I hide you under the zipper bag of wool sweaters in my closet, so not even Tirsa knows.

Dear Lydia,

You have not hurt my feelings, and I sympathize with your frustration at the question that is not a question.

You ask what you would do in church. If you can think of nothing else to do, you can look around for us, for the saints. We are all there, you know. We worship along with you who are still on earth.

Tirsa is God's child just as you and I are, and I am delighted by your picture of her as a wise little owl. No doubt she is wise. Many children know more about God than a college full of scholars could.

Whatever strange and frightful thing you are imagining, Tirsa is correct that you will not find it in the Eucharist. When you love someone, what do you wish most? You wish to be close to the person you love. It is the same with God. He wishes to be close to you and to each human being in His creation. So He comes to us in a form we can assimilate. The church is the place where God is known and loved, so the church is where we go to receive Him, in the simple way He gave us Himself.

Some things are only frightening if you do not understand them.

Content to remain your secret friend under the sweaters,
Saint Lydia

July 18

Dear Saint Lydia,

I didn't go to church, and I know my parents wish I had. It's been less than two months since they were baptized, and already they're impatient for me to convert, even though this is supposed to be my choice. What that really means is that I can take my time as long as I choose what they want me to choose in the end.

I decided to spend the morning with my Aunt Aven because Aunt Aven doesn't go to church either. I think she used to go, but she doesn't now. She works for the government and raises cocker spaniels. She was married, a long time ago, but her husband was killed in a car accident a block away from their apartment. I always thought it would have been better if he was killed far away, on some big highway on a long road trip somewhere, so she wouldn't have to feel like he almost made it home.

Aunt Aven is nice. We made blueberry pancakes and played with the puppies. She didn't bug me about not going to church or ask what my parents were up to or anything. She's my mom's older sister, but she's the quiet one of the two. Probably people say that about me and Tirsa, although Tirsa is not as *vivacious* as Mom. She just likes to talk more than I do.

All those pancakes made me sleepy.

Off to take an afternoon nap,

Lydia

P.S. Do saints ever appear to people in dreams?

Dear Lydia,

We do indeed appear to people in dreams, and we appear to people when they are wide awake as well. You would be surprised to see me walking into your room one day to speak with you, but many people have received such visits, from me and from countless others more holy than I am.

Does your aunt know that her husband still lives, here in this world where we go after death? Does she know that Christian marriage is eternal? Perhaps if she returned to church, she would feel closer to her husband. She is bound to him in a mystery, in Christ, and one day, with His grace, they will lead one another into the kingdom of God. The time of his death, even the fact of his death, cannot affect this.

I pray that you will know eternal love, as it was meant for you.

In Christ our beloved Savior,

Saint Lydia

10

Dear Saint Lydia,

Jill called this afternoon, and she said she decided to call Trella herself. Jill makes people laugh so easily that sometimes, she can handle awkward situations better than we can because she does it so lightly. She has such a good sense of people and how they're responding to her, and she can switch from serious to silly quickly if someone's getting tense.

She said Trella wouldn't talk to her either. Trella told her that she really is sick to her stomach, and that she's glad we all care about her, but nothing is going on, and she's sure she will be better soon.

Which is a sure sign that something *is* going on. Whenever someone tells you that nothing is going on, you can count on something disastrous happening in the near future. What's worse is that Trella is saying "nothing" to *us*. If she can't tell *us* about whatever it is, she can't tell *anyone*.

If this were anyone on earth except Trella, I would almost wonder if she was pregnant. I know I shouldn't even be saying this, but when someone suddenly becomes moody, nauseated, and unwilling to talk about her boyfriend, it's only human to wonder. But I can't imagine Trella doing anything so . . . *accidental*. Trella is destined to graduate first in her class from Harvard Law on the day she accepts her nomination to be the first female president of the United States. Or she might get the Nobel Prize for curing cancer while still in grad school. What she won't be doing is getting pregnant at seventeen with a guy who is virtually unknown to her best friends and therefore can't possibly be The One.

Men are way more trouble than they're worth, if you ask me.

Which doesn't explain why I'm now going downstairs to watch a romantic movie. I wonder why love stories are so much more appealing than actual "lovers."

Lydia

Dear Lydia,

What dissatisfaction you seem to feel when you contemplate the race of men! Your father does not stand up for himself, Paul is an egomaniac, Chad was never part of the group, and now you have condemned the entire gender as more trouble than they are worth. Have you considered that in all three cases, there may be good reasons for the characteristics you dislike? Your father may not assert his wishes about "the little issues" because he feels they are not important. Paul may appear to be an egotist because he has not learned yet how to manage his intellectual gifts. Chad may not have joined your group because you never made him feel welcome. Strive to see the other person's viewpoint on the world before you pass such ready judgment.

A man is a person, dear girl, just as you are. And despite the many obstacles erected between men and women by the world in which you live, the two sexes in their original state are the perfect complement to one another (one might even say the perfect antidote, in some senses). Human beings were not created in the jumbled state in which you often find them. When God created humanity, He looked upon His creation and found it good, male and female. It is left to us to find our way back to this original perfection, to the masculinity and femininity for which we were intended, in the image and likeness of our Creator.

The balance between maintaining protective boundaries and condemning all men out of hand can be difficult to maintain. One man may be the greatest danger the earth holds for you, and another will be your companion in eternal confidence and joy. It takes practice to learn discernment in approaching men so that you are able to protect yourself against the evil ones without destroying your chance of knowing and trusting the one good man you will one day marry.

I will leave you to learn about Trella in God's time. When you have lived longer, you will know that being organized does not protect a person from all misfortunes. Indeed, a person who believes her life to be completely in her own control may be blinded to her weaknesses and thereby become a victim of them.

And the reason love stories are so much more appealing than real men is that they are fictional and are largely derived from the hopeful fantasies we all fall prey to, not from the living experience of real love. The more one focuses on creating romance for its own sake, the farther one strays from the personal discipline and perception that open hearts to one another. Romantic stories tell us that love will solve all our problems and meet all our needs. In reality, we enter a loving relationship to serve more than to be served. There is an irreconcilable difference between these two objectives.

In Christ who served us,
Saint Lydia

11

July 24

Dear Saint Lydia,

It's a rainy Saturday afternoon. I'm curled up on top of my big bureau next to the window. I have a cushion, a cup of tea with honey, and my journal. I'm watching raindrops slide down the glass. This is a built-in window that doesn't open, so there's no screen. Just me on one side and the rain on the other, and only the glass between.

I wish it was like that with God. Only a glass between, so I could see through.

Church is never like a glass because it's cluttered up with people. Church people make me itch. Take the Sampsons, our next-door neighbors. The Sampsons are a bundle of laughs. They go to one of those hardline churches where they think everyone but them is going to hell. For years, they were after my parents to "get saved" so we wouldn't go to hell.

Now, my parents have joined a church, and the Sampsons don't know what to do. At first, they were thrilled to bits, but then they found out what kind of church it was, and they were so confused. They like that word "Christian" in the title, but they've never heard of this kind of Christian, and when they see my mom crossing herself or not eating meat on Friday, it looks like Catholicism to them. They think the Catholic Church is evil. Yikes!

What is so great about believing everyone but you is going to hell? What are you saying about God if you think that's what He wants people to believe? I'm not convinced that He does.

I will now make a list of everything that irritates me about church people. I still can't believe that my own family could technically belong on this list . . .

1. Too many church people think their way is the only way.
2. Too many of them are nice to you because they think they should be, not because they want to be.
3. They always have an agenda. They never talk to you without secretly wishing to convince you of their views.
4. They don't care about the environment because they think the world is coming to an end.
5. They think sex is the only really important sin.
6. They think you can get saved once and all your problems will end. Ha.

This is a funny thing to be telling you. You must be a religious person. However, you have not yet done any of these things in my presence, so to be fair, I won't hold you guilty of them until you do.

Sigh.

I don't know what I think I'm accomplishing here.

Do you know what really bothers me?

The way things are, if I ever did want to become Orthodox, it would be a victory for my parents. It would be me giving in to them. It's not that they're The Great Oppressors, or anything like that. It's just that they keep telling me how great it would be if I got baptized, and that makes it about pleasing them. I won't ever be able to feel confident in my faith if I'm always wondering if I just gave in to the pressure.

I wish it could be the same way for me that it was for you. One day, Saint Paul told you all about it, and you liked what he said, so you got baptized and then had him over for dinner.

The rain has stopped. I can see gardens through the glass, and green leaves dancing in the breeze, scattering raindrops on the wet grass. I'm going outside. I'm tired of looking at all this beauty through a closed window.

Lydia

Dear Lydia,

No two people in history have ever been alike. Your spirit is your own, and only your own spiritual journey will bring you to God. However many women share our name, you are the only Lydia, the only you. Until you came, your particular share of creation stood empty, waiting for fulfillment in your birth. Creation could not have been complete without you, or without any individual human soul that has been born or will be born in time to come.

Open the window, dear girl. Don't worry about whether you are giving in to your parents. Set them aside completely and open the window for yourself, for your own satisfaction. Remember, there is only one Lydia. Your faith cannot depend upon another person's qualities or actions, and your individuality was given to you by God and will not crumble away if you do not wish it to.

Stop thinking of your faith in terms of your parents' faith. Stop thinking of it as something they have asked you to do or as a way of rejoining the family group. God asked you before they did, and He will go on asking you long after they have ceased to have any authority in your life.

That being said, I commend your effort in making the list of what annoys you about church people, as you call them. It is helpful to examine what troubles you, as a first step toward resolution. And I do appreciate your fairness in refusing to condemn me of any of these failings until I give you just cause.

Your list is accurate in many senses, but it misses the same point that you are missing when you think of your parents. Whom you find in a church has nothing to do with your own reason for being there. God is present, no matter how many irritating human beings are praying next to you, and the saints are there, praying for all of you, irritating or not.

Talk to God yourself, Lydia. Like me, He has been talking to you since long before you showed any signs of hearing Him.

With prayers and exhortations,

Saint Lydia

July 31

Dear Saint Lydia,

Here's a strange thought. No, wait, let me start the story from the beginning and then you can have my strange thought.

This weekend, we went to my mother's first cousin's wedding. Her name is Lorinda, and this is *not* her first marriage. I think this was number three, although there was a boyfriend in there who lasted a while . . . did she marry him . . . I'm not sure. But you get the picture.

As an aside, I wonder why Mom still goes to her weddings. The first time, you go because it's your cousin. The second time, you go because you hope this time will be better than last time. But the third time? Are you still thinking Lorinda is going to permanently marry *anyone*?

Lorinda's invitation said, "Ned, Nora, Lydia and friend, and Tirsa and friend," so I asked Lauren to come with me because we were going to do something together that day anyhow. Of course, I'm sure Lorinda meant for me to bring a boy, but I have *no* interest in being the object of bad jokes about my supposed love-life.

Even having Lauren with me, I was in a bad mood because I don't like Lorinda. She has a loud laugh when nothing is funny, and she keeps winking and pinching at you as if almost every word you say is a sexual reference and she's the only one who gets it. This would all be bad enough, but she does this in front of my parents and friends, which is so stupid it's embarrassing. She thinks she's being "hip" and staying in touch with my generation, but speaking for my generation, we think she's a freak. She should be what she is—about 50 and getting married *way* too often. She definitely cannot be what we are.

But, as I was saying, Mom thinks it's supportive of Lorinda's better self if we all keep going to her weddings, no matter how many she has, so off we go, wearing nice clothes and nice manners and wishing we were anywhere else on earth. Lauren kept making comments that sounded like she was watching a sideshow at the circus. I've told her about Lorinda, but she couldn't believe a real person could be like that, and I think she was actually hoping Lorinda would do something shocking (more shocking, that is, than marrying for the third time in seven years). If Lauren was related to someone like Lorinda, she wouldn't think it was so funny.

So there I was in the pew of whatever church this was, getting a headache from sitting next to the pew bouquet of overpoweringly smelly pink lilies. I decided to try to think about something else. I couldn't talk to Lauren during the service, so I let my mind wander off, and I started thinking about marriage. *Not* in the Lorinda sense of something you do every two years whether you need to or not.

I mean marriage, true love, universal permission to have sex . . . and then what? What is it really? What is getting married? My parents are married, but it's hard to look at them and imagine them being in love. I mean, they must have been in love to get married, but they're my parents.

I just can't imagine them having emotions I would consider romantic.

But while I was thinking about them, my strange thought struck me. My mother was giving me the updated version of her "men and women" talk the other day. I say "updated" because she's changed it since she became Orthodox. She still doesn't want me to have sex unless I'm married, but now she says that marriage is eternal. *Eternal.* She says it's a mystery in Christ and that I and my husband will be bonded together forever and lead one another into the kingdom of God.

On the one hand, if this is true, it's a huge motivation to pick the right man: Once you have him, you're stuck with him. On the other hand, I suddenly thought my strange thought. Mom and Dad weren't Orthodox when they met, married, had two kids . . . or did anything else they did before this year. So that means they didn't know their marriage would be eternal when they got married. Other Christians think you are married only until you die (or until one of you commits adultery). Not the Orthodox. So now she and Dad are signed up for eternity. Did they know this when they converted? I wonder what they thought. Were they glad? I know this is a horrible question, Saint Lydia, but at least give me credit for asking you instead of asking my mom.

What is it like to suddenly discover that you will be with someone for eternity? Forever and ever and ever, that's it, that's your future.

I have no idea. I guess it makes my parents happy, because no one wants to lose the person they love. Maybe if I had ever been married, I would know how they're feeling. Or how I might feel if I were in the same situation.

I like boys. Except the ones who are idiots. Sometimes, I have liked boys a lot. But seriously, what high school crush is going to stand up to me walking around going, "Do I want to be with this boy to eternity?"

And then, as I'm sitting on the pew and staring into space, deep in my reverie, I realize that *Paul* is sitting two pews ahead of me on the other side of the aisle. Wearing a suit and cufflinks! I almost choked! No more reverie for me. He was on the groom's side, so he must be a friend or relative of Lorinda's latest. I slid as far down behind the monstrous pew bouquet as I could. Lauren raised her eyebrows at me and kept hissing, "What? What?" but I just told her I had a muscle cramp and had to shift position. I know my luck. If Lauren had seen Paul and decided we should say hi to him after the service, Lorinda would have swooped down out of nowhere and tried to make something out of nothing. No, thank you. I would rather run over my own foot with a lawnmower.

Fortunately, I escaped unnoticed. I came home to tea and Advil, and called Jill so she could make me laugh about Lorinda. But it wasn't a satisfying phone call, because it was too embarrassing to tell her about my Paul panic (and she would tell Lauren, and then Lauren would bring it up . . . *Ack*!). And I couldn't tell her about my strange thought either, because I still don't talk about The Religious Situation with my friends. I'm sure they would either take it too seriously or not seriously enough, and I don't feel like adding their freakouts to my list of personal burdens. I almost told Maria Louisa once, because she's Catholic, but that's just it—she *is* Catholic, and so's her whole family, so would she really understand my problem?

So I wrote to you instead.

I've written you so many letters now that you're becoming a person in my mind. I wonder if my imaginary Saint Lydia is anything like your real self was. Or is.

Good night,
Lydia

Dear Lydia,

The answer to all of this is love. True love cannot permit itself to be anything but eternal. On earth, there is never time enough, even if you live to be a hundred years old, to live out your love for one another. If you have married from your true heart, purely and in ecstasy and with deep good sense, you can never have too much time together, to learn from one another, to quarrel and repent, to grieve and rediscover one another after grief, to lose your inherent selfishness in desire to spare each other pain, to become free of the need to control one another, to understand without speaking more than a single glance.

If your parents love one another, their conversion brought them relief from a burden they have carried from the moment they fell in love. All human beings fear death, but those who love others fear it most of all. For them, death without faith would be a double loss, a loss of self and of everyone and everything they have loved. Without faith, death is the loss of an entire world. With faith, death gains us the world without end.

I can understand your reluctance to tell your friends about your thoughts, but I must also tell you, dear girl, that you are beginning to create an island for yourself in your troubles, and one day the island will become unbearable. You are an island in your family, the one who was "left behind" when the conversion took place, and as you open your mind increasingly to the wider world of the spirit, you are becoming an island among your friends, moving away from them because you feel you cannot take them on your journey. You may be right, but if this proves to be the case, what are your plans for finding new friends? Where might you look for good friends with whom you can share all the facets of your life?

As for your mother's cousin, I believe fear of death is her trouble, too. She is so afraid to die that she seeks to arrest her own maturity, as if that could stop time. Her anxiety prevents her from settling deeply into anything, least of all marriage. A person who cannot accept the passage of time with equanimity will never be able to accept the labor of a lasting love.

You are strongly in my mind at this moment, dear Lydia.

In prayer and meditation,

Saint Lydia

August 3

Dear Saint Lydia,

It's me again. It's after midnight. I woke up in the middle of a very intense dream that you were writing back to all my letters, right in this journal. It was so clear. I could see the pages with your letters on them, but I couldn't read them because it was so dark in my room. It really is dark in my room, it's the middle of the night, and when I woke up I was still so caught up in my dream that I went scrabbling around in the closet, throwing the sweaters on the floor to get to my journal. I was so sure I would open it and find letters from you. I found the journal, and by then I was starting to wake up, so I realized I couldn't read it in the dark, and I turned on my light. At that moment, I knew it had been a dream. But I had to look. I had to open the journal and separate each page and be sure there was nothing hidden, nothing that had not been there all along.

If I had gotten to my journal before I really woke up, would I have seen your letters?

I feel so disappointed, I don't think I can go back to sleep. I was so sure there would be something from you, something to show you read them all, something to show you are real.

It was a dream. It was so intense I thought it was real.

Good night,

Lydia

Dear Lydia,

It was real. You almost saw my letters, but you convinced yourself you couldn't see them as you woke up.

I understand your disappointment. It is mutual.

With love,

Saint Lydia

August 7

Dear Saint Lydia,

Today, I am 18 years old. Last year, for my seventeenth birthday party, we had a big barbeque in the backyard with all the girls from my volleyball team. My friends gave me great presents, and I got a car key with a pink ribbon tied to it from Mom and Dad because their present was (*finally!*) letting me learn to drive. Now all I need is a car of my own and enough money to pay for gas and insurance.

This year, my family is Orthodox, so my birthday is in the middle of the Dormition fast, the two weeks of fasting before the feast day when they celebrate the Dormition of the Theotokos (which means the day Mary, the Mother of God, went to heaven). I asked Tirsa why they call it Dormition, and she knew. She always knows this stuff, even though she's only six. She said "dormition" means going to sleep. That's what they say when someone dies, because of eternal life. They say the person went to sleep in the Lord, or something like that, because their soul didn't die, just their body. But you already know all that.

Mom and Dad asked me what I'd like to do about my birthday. They said I could celebrate it before or after the fast, so we could have another barbeque or whatever else I might want that included meat and dairy products, or we could celebrate on the day itself and Mom would just make two sets of food, fasting food for them and whatever I wanted for me and anyone I chose to invite. Is this what will happen to my birthday every year if I get baptized? No more birthday cake? Well, no, Mom has a great "fasting" chocolate cake recipe, so at least I could still have cake. I guess it's not a big deal, but it's frustrating to run into their Orthodoxy at every turn, even on my birthday. Not only that, it means that if I invite my friends, I'll have to explain to them why there are two menus and why my own family isn't eating my birthday cake. Unless it's a fasting birthday cake. Would they know it was? Would they care?

I went off by myself and stressed out for a while. It's so aggravating! Why can't anything go smoothly any more? Why is *my* birthday about *their* religion? Eventually, I wore myself out, gave up on being angry, and decided to make the best of things. The only other option would be to cut my family out completely and go party somewhere with my friends, but frankly, it would be more trouble than it's worth. More drama with my parents is *not* what I want for my birthday. I'm burned out.

So I decided to have a nice candlelit dinner at home, with my family, Aunt Aven, and my two cousins I've never told you about who live near us and know all about The Religious Situation. And I told Tirsa she could invite Rachel, her new Best-Friend-Forever from the church where she and my parents go.

The birthday dinner was nice. I told myself to chill out and just *be there*. I made up my mind to make it a good memory because I don't want to look back at my eighteenth birthday and feel bitter. I made a vow in the morning not to think about anything at all until tomorrow, and I think I pulled it off—at least until now, when I decided to write to you. But the day's over, so I've met my goal.

I've been thinking too much, I think. Ever since my parents converted, I've been thinking and thinking and thinking. I analyze everything that happens in our family and everything that happens in my own experience. I can't seem to stop. I can't seem to look at life just as life going by anymore. Everything has a meaning, and I can't stop trying to find it. I want to know what the truth is. I want to go on shaking things and poking around and listening at keyholes all over the universe until I know I've seen *what is*. What really and truly *is*. Then I will be content.

I want to climb right out of my hyperactive brain. I want to be away from the same old awkward conversations with my parents and the same old avoided conversations with my friends. This is a big reason I'm so ready to leave for college. I want to stretch my wings, Saint Lydia. I want to try out my life in a completely new setting. I want some room to think, or room to stop thinking too much.

I need someone to talk to. I know I have you. Sometimes you're so real to me I could swear I can almost hear you. But I can't hear you. Not really. I need to talk to someone I can see. Maybe at college I will make new friends I can really talk to, people who haven't known me so long they don't know me at all, people who will see me just as I am, right now, with no context except myself.

But don't worry, Saint Lydia. I will still write to you. I think I would miss these letters, even without being able to see your answers. If there are any.

Love,

Lydia

Dear Lydia,

That is good news, dear girl. It would grieve me also to lose you.

You give me great hope for your future today, my newly 18-year-old friend. It is good and right that you should wish to travel the universe in search of what is. The Holy Trinity, our God, is what is. The more you seek earnestly for this, the closer you will come to Him. And when you finally peer through the right keyhole and see Him, you will indeed be content.

I know you sometimes feel that you are making yourself crazy with so much thinking, and that is certainly possible, but I do not think you have harmed yourself yet. You have told me of your struggles with suspecting your parents of speaking to you from ulterior motives, however benevolent these motives may be, and you have told me of your reluctance to speak of your inner life with your friends. Perhaps it is God's will that you step out of your familiar contexts and try your wings this year at college, where you will not feel so hard-pressed and may be free to explore your faith without emotional distractions.

When you step out of what is familiar to you, be careful to choose wisely what you will leave behind and what you will take with you. Doubts and pressures certainly can be left, but you must choose something to stand for your faith, something to keep your face turned upward until you have found the Strength Itself upon which you can rely. So many people step out into the world and drown in its hideous entanglements, never suspecting their own weakness or the deep and sinister darkness that lurks behind apparent ecstasy. If you cannot yet see God, at least choose what is good in what you love and cling to it with all your might. Let nothing wrest it from your grasp, lest you find yourself being swept away.

As for your birthday celebration, I must say that although I respect your parents' dedication, I also understand your frustration. Your parents, like many new believers, are glowing with zealous love for Orthodoxy, and they are a little blind at the moment to the effects of this vigorous enthusiasm on their daughter who cannot yet share it. It seems to me that your birthday should have been an occasion for relaxing the new ways a little to remind you that what is happening to you is still as important as what is happening to them. I will pray that God will grant them a patient and merciful perception of your experiences.

Nevertheless, I am pleased to see you making the best of a difficult situation, and I believe that no matter how you resolve the religious differences in your family, you need not worry too much about how your birthday will be celebrated in the coming years. There are wonderful recipes for "fasting birthday cake," and as you grow older, you will care less for the external features of the celebration than for the joy of sharing it with loved ones. And no doubt you will soon realize that birthday gifts are not subject to the rules of fasting! For example, did learning to drive involve eating meat and cheese?

With love and best wishes for the coming year,
Saint Lydia

15

August 9

Dear Saint Lydia,

I've had a hard day.

Our town has a lake with a sandy beach around it, and there's a summer beach volleyball league that plays at the lake. They're mostly just pick-up games, and we make teams out of whoever shows up, but there are a lot of us who come every year, and my friends and I have been coming since we were freshmen. We always skip the first summer session because it's right after school, but we always play in August. This year, we'll have to miss the end of the August session for college, but we decided to play as long as we could, just this one last time. Usually, it's a blast. We're at the beach all day on game days, swimming, picnicking, and just lying in the sand, watching the people go by and laughing about nothing. But not today.

Mom and Tirsa had to be somewhere today, so I rode to the beach with Jill and Maria Louisa. While we were still getting our stuff out of the car, we saw Trella sitting on a bench near the parking lot. She didn't have her game bag, and she wasn't dressed to play. She must have been watching for us, because when she saw us coming, she stood up and waited for us to get to her. And then, before any of us could even say hello, she told us she's pregnant and she doesn't feel well enough to play in the beach league, and she won't be going to college with us this year after all.

She got through her whole little speech, told us she loves us and will miss us, and then she sat down and started crying. Maria Louisa sat down with her, took Trella's face in her hands, and said, "Don't you let them take your baby. No matter how bad they make you feel, don't you let them take it away. You be the mama now. You can get through this, and I will get through it with you." Then she put her arms around Trella, and Trella cried on her shoulder, right there in the parking lot, broken-hearted.

I couldn't think of anything to say. I was too stunned. I patted Trella's back once or twice and felt helpless. Finally, I dragged Jill off to the beach and left Maria Louisa to do what we couldn't. In a little while, Maria Louisa came too. We didn't say anything to each other. We were all afraid to say the wrong thing, even among ourselves.

The rest of the team showed up and we started warming up for the game, but none of us girls played very well today because we couldn't concentrate on anything but Trella, sitting there on the bench, waiting for her mom to pick her up, with her head down and Kleenex in her hand.

It's not that I'm shocked to learn that sex goes on in high school. Who doesn't know that? But you have to understand who Trella is. She has a future all mapped out for herself, and she does everything the right way the first time. She's the best volleyball player our high school has seen for years. She won a scholarship for college because she's so smart. She's attractive in every sense, and people love to be around her. I'm sure the hardest thing she ever had to tell her parents before this was, "I got an A– instead of an A+." Her parents must have gone through the roof. She looks like she's been crying for days.

I keep thinking about what Maria Louisa said to Trella, about not letting anyone make her give up on that baby. I know she meant "don't let them make you get an abortion." Maria Louisa is Super Catholic. She's the oldest of six children, and she was there when the last two were born. She knows everything there is to know about human reproduction, but not the way the "bad girls" know it. She knows it the way it's meant to work, when it all goes the right way. That makes her sound kind of wimpy and sheltered, but she isn't like that at all. She's totally practical, and in some ways, she seems older than the rest of us. I guess having five siblings has aged her!

Trella's parents must be furious. I wonder what makes them angrier, the fact that she had sex or the fact that she got pregnant. Her parents are successful, professional people who expect their hard work to pay off. Usually, it does. Her father's a judge and her mother's a college professor. I don't think they go to church. It might be unfair of me, but I'm guessing they're most angry because she wasn't "careful" about having sex. She didn't prepare correctly, and now her life is over.

But the baby is a human baby, not a contraception error. None of this is the baby's fault. Who is speaking up for the baby? Maria Louisa is, but who else? Are her parents? If Trella keeps the baby, her parents will have to help her, because she doesn't have a job and she isn't married. Are they willing to help her? Would they really pressure her to abort her baby? Maybe they want her to put the baby up for adoption. Wouldn't it be hard to give up your baby forever, to never see it again or know what kind of life it has? But at least it would be better than abortion. At least with adoption, you know the baby is alive.

Can Trella ever play volleyball again? Can she go to college next year, after the baby is born? Maybe she could if she gives up the baby, but what if she doesn't want to give up the baby?

I just thought of something else. If she keeps the baby, she's going to have to let her parents help her raise it. She's dependent on them. But can you imagine letting your parents raise your kid? I would hate that! No offense to my parents, but I have plans. When I'm a mom, I'm going to do things my way, not their way. But maybe Trella won't have a choice.

You know what makes this even worse? Jill told us on the way home in the car that she heard from Janina, the one on our high school team who always has the dirt on everyone, that Trella and Chad got into a big fight at a party about two weeks ago, and he broke up with her. So now Trella's got a baby and no boyfriend. I'm sure he's the father, but he doesn't care, so where does that get her? This is like a picture with a bunch of pieces cut out of it. There's a mom and a baby, but no dad, no house, no job . . . it's not supposed to work like this.

But that's still not the baby's fault.

Well, she wouldn't have told us all she was pregnant if she wasn't going to have the baby. But will she keep it? I wonder what the baby will look like. What will she name it? I hope it's already born by the time we come home on spring break so we can see it. A baby is a baby, no matter what.

In fact, I think I'll round up our old team and get them to throw a baby shower for Trella, maybe over Christmas break or something. Maria Louisa will help me. But first I'll have to find out if Trella's going to keep the baby. It would be awful to throw a shower for her and then find out that she can't keep the baby.

I'm exhausted.

Love,

Lydia

Dear Lydia,

I am sure you are exhausted, dear girl. You have had so much to think about and so much to feel in such a short space of time. You are sad for your friend and troubled by your own musings over her situation.

You have the most important point solved. A baby is a baby, no matter what. A baby is a new human being created lovingly by God in His image. The circumstances under which the baby was conceived make no difference at all to the baby's value. God spends just as much loving attention on creating babies born out of wedlock as He does on the most respectably conceived child.

Maria Louisa is a good friend to Trella. The most important thing Trella can do right now is to keep herself and her baby healthy throughout her pregnancy and to become the best mother she is able to be. It is true that she has made a serious mistake, and she has certainly earned the frustration and grief she has caused for herself and her family. But she will redeem herself by bearing and raising this baby with all the love and intelligence she can muster. This is her chance to use her many gifts for something that matters far more than volleyball or high marks at school. It is to be hoped that her parents will support her efforts in healthy ways.

It is true that in some instances, the most loving thing a mother can do is to offer her baby up for adoption by people who will be able to care for her baby better than she would herself. Perhaps she has no family or friends to support her as she raises her child, or perhaps she knows that she will be unable to give her baby a safe and loving home, and a chance to make better choices than she may have made in her own life. Whatever her circumstances, when a woman makes this choice honestly and from love, it is a pure and precious sacrifice. But I believe in Trella's case, Maria Louisa is right. Trella has become a mother, and her salvation lies in clinging to this fact with all her strength.

There is a destructive illusion abroad in the world that abortion creates a choice for the mother, that it retrieves her former life for her, so that she can go on as if the pregnancy had never happened. This is a complete falsehood.

The truth is that Trella's former life was gone forever the moment she became pregnant. No matter what she chose after that, there was no choice open to her that did not involve lifelong consequences. Physical termination of a pregnancy does nothing to erase the fact of the pregnancy itself. The pregnancy will either produce a baby, or it will produce lifelong bondage to painful regret over an act that can never be undone. No amount of grief and remorse will revive a tiny heart that has ceased to beat. Trella's body, her mind, and her soul will always remember that a new life began inside her. Only by nurturing that life will she regain her peace and recover freedom from regret. One must work with God's order, not against it, to achieve delight and fruitful living.

Although it may be difficult, I hope that you will find ways to remain friends with Trella, and to keep her company through her pregnancy and as she begins to raise her baby. She will have many hard days, and she will often feel the loss of her old life, especially because she will likely lose some of her old friends. I hope you will not be one of the friends she loses, dear girl. I hope that you will be someone who supports all her efforts to make something good and precious out of her shattered life.

With prayers for you all and especially for the baby,
Saint Lydia

16

August 9, Again

Dear Saint Lydia,

I feel rotten. I just walked out of a big fight with my mom at the point where she said, "Lydia Jane, if you can't listen to what I say, you can't tell me you know what I think. Every person is a mystery, known fully only by God, so stop making assumptions and imposing them on me!"

I could have said the same thing to her. I should have said it. But I was too mad to think it up in the heat of the moment.

The fight started because I told my mom about Trella when I got home from the volleyball game. Immediately, she started in on how Trella made a bad choice and now it's going to wreck her life, and when I tried to show the other side of the case, she said I clearly thought what Trella did was great. Just because I tried to say that I thought it was more important to support her and the baby now than to spend time harping on what she should have done in the past. It's like my mom thinks teenage pregnancy is contagious and I'll catch it too if she doesn't make me hate Trella.

I *know* Trella's life is a wreck. I really do! I have no plans to race out and get pregnant. Matter of fact, I'm not even having sex (and it's not because I've never had the chance!), so what is my mom trying to say about me? Either she thinks I'm weak or she doesn't trust me, or she thinks I'm too young (at 18!) to understand what happened. It makes me so mad.

The thing is, if my mom had started the conversation as a conversation, instead of being so anxious and accusing, maybe I would have felt like I could talk to her about Trella and the mess she's made of her life. Maybe I did sound like I thought it was okay, but that's just because I don't think it helps anyone to condemn Trella to hell and walk away.

My mom said that if you tell yourself often enough that it's okay to have premarital sex, you will start to believe it. I'm sure she has a point. Behavior can be contagious. Kind of like how you start talking with a Southern accent when you're around someone who has a Southern accent. You don't even think about it. Your mouth just starts doing it. But this is *sex* we're talking about. Sex and a real live *baby*. Am I really going to just "slip" into that? And I *wasn't* saying it was okay. I don't think Trella thinks it was such a great idea either. I was just saying that isn't the point now if I'm going to be a good friend to Trella and her baby.

I hate fighting with my mom. I hate what she does that makes me want to fight with her, but she's still my mom and I hate fighting with her. I hate that we always butt heads and talk past each other instead of talking like sane human beings.

So Mom is a mystery, is she? Fine. This sounds like Orthodox talk to me, but I can see it's true. People are mysteries. How many people actually know what I think and feel? Even if I tell them myself, how well can I actually describe what goes on inside me? Sometimes I don't have the right words. Sometimes I don't figure out what I mean until it's too late to say anything. Sometimes I can sense whole parts of me as a human being that I've never explored because I've never been in situations where they would be needed. For example, I could theoretically be a mom some day (*not* in my teens!), but what kind of mom would I be? What would I think and feel as a mom? What would I do? Even I don't know that yet, because I've never been a mom.

What don't I know about my mom? What parts of the mystery have I not unraveled? What would I know about her if I wasn't mad at her fifty percent of the time? What could we tell each other if I was her own age and she respected me? Would I have been friends with her when she was 18? Why can't I know her outside this one context of her being my mom?

What if she could be inside my head for a day, looking out at the world as me, thinking my thoughts, feeling my feelings, noticing what I notice, reacting like I react? What if I could be her? Would we decide that we were worse than we thought, or would we suddenly be able to love each other like never before?

I bet the world would look wildly complicated if we could see all the millions of worlds that it actually is, viewed through all the individual pairs of eyes that look out on it.

What would you do if you were me? Should I go out there and apologize? Will I accomplish anything, or will we just get mad all over again?

Ugh.

Love,

Lydia

Dear Lydia,

I am sorry for your distress. You have asked what I would do if I were you. Only you will ever be you, but I can make a suggestion of what to do next. I can see you fear that any apology will be seen as an admission of weakness and will encourage your mother to continue treating you like a child. The answer, in this case, seems to be to show her you are not a child. When you are able to do so calmly (and this may take some time), find your mother and tell her what is wrong. Tell her that you wish you could explain to her how you actually feel about Trella but that you feel like you cannot talk to her because she is not giving you the chance. Show her that your judgment is more mature than she thinks it is by describing what you have in common in your views of Trella's situation, and then ask her respectfully to give you the chance to speak next time before she makes assumptions about what you will say.

In fairness to your mother, I am sure you gave her evidence of something less than maturity in the course of this argument. No doubt she also regrets some of what she said or did, and she is likely wondering how she can communicate this to you without undermining her authority as your parent and your guardian and protector.

The transition from making all your choices for you out of deep love and a need to protect you to the day when she will hand all responsibility over to you as you enter womanhood yourself is bound to be difficult. Her role in your life is changing, but her love for you will not change. Mother-love is so deep and so powerful it defies description. Find an icon of the Holy Mother of God cradling her Infant Redeemer in her arms. Consider what extreme joy and pain she must have felt as His mother, watching Him die a horrible death to save all of humanity, including herself, and then seeing Him come to life again, defeating death. Imagine watching the person dearest to you endure such things. Look at her face pressed against His baby cheek and have mercy on your own mother, as your own child must one day have mercy on you for the same tight grip of love.

As to the human mystery, dear girl, you are more Orthodox than you know. You have said it. You are a mystery even to yourself, and if each human being could see through the eyes of others, much of the misery on earth would vanish.

With love,
Saint Lydia

August 11

Dear Saint Lydia,

I thought about it for two days and then decided that my mom will only see me as an adult if I show her clearly that I *am* an adult (and even then it might not happen!). So I thought about what I could say to her about our fight that would be okay with me. I chose to tell her I was sorry that our conversation turned into a fight, but that I felt like she didn't give me a chance before she took my head off. I don't know whether I did a good job of saying all this because it was hard not to get angry all over again, but it didn't turn into an actual fight this time, so that's something.

Although she said that her judgment is going to be part of my life for a while yet, whether I like it or not, she did listen when I told her that if she is a mystery, so am I. She didn't say anything for a little while, maybe because she was trying to decide what to say. Then she said, "Do you know what was the biggest hurdle I had to cross to become Orthodox?" I said, "No, I don't." She said, "I should have told you more about my journey." This made me uncomfortable, because I couldn't tell if she meant that she should have talked to me more as if I would understand, or if she was just thinking that maybe if she had talked to me differently about the decision-making, it would have persuaded me to become Orthodox. I hate that I'm always wondering if she's just talking to me or if she's talking to me with an agenda. I've decided that persuasion should never be part of human relationships, and I don't care if that's not a practical opinion!

So then I said, "Well, are you going to tell me what the hurdle was?" And she said the biggest hurdle was when she learned that the only way to really know God is to love Him. This sounds like a pretty simple statement, but the more you think about it, the less simple it becomes. It's not how people approach relationships with other people. We get to know other people and *then* decide if we love them or not. But she said you have to *start* with love, or you can't know God.

Hmmmm. I know God is not the same as a human being, but this still seems a little unreasonable to me. How do I know I would love Him if I don't know Him? How can I love what I don't know? Can't I at least know a little bit about Him before I decide to love Him? How will I know what I'm loving if I don't know Him until I love Him?

And what does this have to do with our fight over Trella? Maybe she was making an analogy about us, about how we didn't trust each other and that was why we couldn't hear each other.

Perplexed as usual,

Lydia

P.S. I was thinking that if God appeared to me like He appeared to people in Bible times, then it would solve everything. But I'm guessing that doesn't happen except to people who love Him.

Dear Lydia,

In truth, God appears to those who love Him and to those who do not. Consider Saint Paul, the man who converted me and did so much to build the original Christian Church. God appeared to him at a time when he was notorious for persecuting Christians. The experience changed Saint Paul's life forever, but you certainly cannot say that he already loved God when it happened. Indeed, he was doing his best to work against Him!

But you may still be right that it would not solve anything for you. You wish for God to appear to you because you think it would free you from the work of going to find Him yourself. If this is the case, you may be sure God knows it, and perhaps He knows that you will only find Him if you do it yourself. Think about yourself, Lydia. What kind of faith would you have created if you simply waited until you could see what you believe in, until you did not need any faith to believe in it? Would God appear to someone who only wanted to see Him to spare herself the effort of looking? You wish to have it both ways, to remain in your natural, visible world while reassuring yourself that there is something beyond it. You must be willing to step beyond the familiar, or the familiar is all you will ever know.

Persuasion is a difficult problem, and you are wise to consider it. It often arises from an abuse of power, of one kind or another, and it often degenerates into a selfish urge to control. Although you must use all your senses, physical and spiritual, to read the people around you in the world, it is never wise to trust too implicitly in your reading of another human being. If you feel yourself to be in harm's way, remove yourself by all means, but do not take the further step of rendering a permanent judgment against another human being. Remember that you are a mystery and look upon your fellow humanity as such. You do not know another person's story, not from the inside, and you may be sure that in most cases, you do not know even all the external factors that contribute to his or her behavior and intentions.

In the case of your mother, when she speaks to you, she is likely speaking from both of the motives you have mentioned—her own wish that she had handled the situation differently and her enduring hope that there is something she can do that will bring you to Orthodoxy. Your faith is between you and God, as she will likely recognize, but you must remember that Orthodoxy is precious to her. If she loves you, she wishes all good things to come to you. Whatever her other feelings, this must be part of what drives her to persuade you.

As for knowing God by loving Him, the reason for this is simple. God is love. How else could you know Him, except by living experience of His essence? With another person, knowledge is separated in time and substance from love. With God, there is no separation of knowledge from love. Knowledge of God is love, by definition.

Do not fear perplexity, dear girl. It is a sign of life and growth.

With love,

Saint Lydia

18

August 12

Dear Saint Lydia,

I never write to you about my dad, did you notice? He's on my mind tonight because I'm leaving for college in two days and he offered to help me pack my room, so we spent the afternoon together, boxing things up and visiting. I liked it. He's always around, but he's the quietest of our family, and when it comes to parenting, he seems to defer to my mom. Maybe he thinks she's the expert because Tirsa and I are both female like she is, or maybe it's just his way to let her do what she wants with us.

I wonder who will be the boss in my marriage, if I ever get married. There shouldn't really be a boss, but you know how it is—you can look at a married couple and see who's the stronger personality, who's making things happen their way and who's just going along. In our house, it usually looks like my mom is making the decisions and doing the talking. My dad is a gentle spirit or something, and my mom is outgoing and outspoken, so in some ways, I think he just likes to let her be his "front man."

For some reason, this makes me think about Paul. He seems very different from Dad. I can't see Paul letting anyone be his "front man." Maybe someone smarter than him (if there is such a person) . . . but there are different ways of being smart, and someone might be smarter than him about people, for example, and still not be smarter intellectually. If he and his wife were equally smart but in different ways, maybe they could trade off being in charge, depending on the situation. But would they, I wonder? Or would they fight all the time?

Why do I think this has anything to do with being smart?

But what I meant to tell you was about my dad, and it's interesting to me. Tirsa told me that it was *Dad*, not Mom, who made sure it was my choice whether I would be baptized. There was this day back before they converted when they were going to meet with the priest, and Tirsa went with them, but I was at a volleyball game. On the way home in the car, Tirsa had her headphones on, and they must have thought she was listening to music, so they started talking about getting baptized and what they were going to do about me. (Personally, I think Tirsa often uses her headphones to take a break or to make people think she's not listening. She's not a spy, exactly . . . well, no more than I am when I listen to my parents praying and talking across the hall at night, right? Sometimes it seems like the only way to get the real scoop on anything in our family!) Tirsa reported that Mom was saying that if infants can be baptized, then I certainly should be, because it clearly doesn't require a rational decision to believe. But Dad said, "No, she's too old. She's 17 (which I was because that was months ago), so it would be like forcing an adult to convert. She's too far out of childhood for us to make the decision for her." And Tirsa said he stuck to his guns and wouldn't let Mom talk him down, even when she argued that my soul could be at stake. He told Mom he could understand why she wanted to make me do it, but that it would be wrong and he wouldn't have it.

Well!

I'm trying to remember if I've ever seen him stand up to her like that. I wanted to go hug him when Tirsa told me because it comforted me so much to know he would fight for me like that, but of course, if I had told him, then he would have known that Tirsa was spying on him, and I couldn't break her confidence. What a tangled thing a family can become. Is that just human, or will I be able to have an untangled family when it's my turn to try it?

I wonder.

Lydia

Dear Lydia,

I am deeply interested in your thoughts about your father, but I cannot resist beginning with my observation that this is the fourth time this Paul has found his way into your letters. I wonder if you are aware of this. Take notice of this boy, Lydia. When something unsought keeps recurring in your life, you must explore it to see if it comes from the Holy Spirit.

Perhaps you are not so alone in your family as you had supposed. Although I can understand the need to keep Tirsa's confidence, you may still find a way to talk to your father about The Religious Situation, as you call it, now that you have seen that he may be able to hear you without leaping to persuade you.

Quiet people are often content to let their more outgoing spouses do the talking, but it does not follow that they themselves have nothing to say. Indeed, the absence of speech is sometimes the best recipe for the presence of thought! You must also consider the fact that your parents have many dealings with one another of which you know nothing because you are not a member of their marriage relationship. It is likely that your father has told your mother what his beliefs and feelings are on the subject of child-rearing and that she incorporates them in her actions and decisions. Your father's influence may not be visible to you, but this does not necessarily mean that it is not there.

There is a pattern to things, dear girl. There is Christ our beloved Redeemer, and there is our mother the Holy Church, who is His Bride. There is a union of Christ with His Church, with Christ and His Body. It is a marriage, not in the gendered worldly sense, but in the sense of a fully loving spiritual whole made from two parts bound together in a mystery. Christ is our Head, and we, His Church, are His Body, His living action in the human realm, on earth and in heaven. The Church on earth is called the Church Militant because you are still struggling to be united with Him and enduring temptation and suffering. The Church in heaven is called the Church Triumphant because we are victorious in death; through our Triumphant Savior, we have achieved all joy and peace in union with Christ, who overcame spiritual death for our sake.

A human man and woman who marry are a part of this pattern, the pattern of Christ and His Church. This does not mean that your father is the "boss" of your mother. It means that he is responsible to God for the spiritual leadership of his family, and that he must strive daily to be as Christ to your mother and to you girls.

When I say he must strive to be "as Christ" to you, this does not mean he sets himself up as God. It means he must seek that perfect, Christlike love, the selfless giving of the self. It is the ultimate generosity to his loved ones to seek their good at all times, at whatever personal cost to himself. In return, it is for your mother to embroider this gift onto the fabric of her days, to cherish and explore the many ways she can apply his efforts at wisdom in the work of family life. Many women on earth make the mistake of believing this to be somehow degrading, that they are lessening themselves by following after a man, but this is not the case. It is a tremendous effort of intelligence and creativity to support and foster the spiritual abilities of another human being. Men and women would be lost without each other; the strength of *each is wholly dependent on the strength of the other. There is no separating it, no splitting of this dynamic into discernible parts. There is no dominance in true Christian marriage, and there is no subjection. It is a cooperative effort of shared gifts, and neither is sufficient without the other.*

In contemplation,

Saint Lydia

19

August 16

Dear Saint Lydia,

Somebody in the universe is laughing very hard right now, because guess what? My new roommate at college, my new *randomly selected* roommate, is *Greek Orthodox!* Her name is Eleni Theodasakis, and when I came into the room with all my boxes, there she was, sitting on the bed, listening to happy Greek music and eating these little cookies that look like tiny loaves of braided bread. She told me what they're called, but I don't have an ear for Greek words yet, so I'll have to ask her again before I can tell you. But whatever my ears are doing, I definitely have a mouth for Greek food. The cookies were good!

Eleni is beautiful, in my opinion. She has big sparkling eyes, shiny dark hair, and she is all rounded lines. There are no flat angles on her anywhere. She talked to me the whole time I was unpacking, and somehow, even though she never stopped talking for a single minute, by the end of the afternoon I had told her the whole story of my life. How did she do this? It is a mystery.

So I put you on my dresser because here it doesn't matter. Eleni's dresser is covered with icons, and dried rose petals, and little brass boxes of things. One Saint Lydia on my dresser is nothing by comparison.

I feel happy and sad to be here all at once. It's *amazingly* good to be free to be whoever I make myself and to try out thoughts and feelings in a place where no one is going to be upset about what I'm feeling and thinking. But it's sad to keep remembering all these little details of my life at home that are missing from my life here. I think that even when I go home again for the summer, it will never be quite the same. It will never be permanent, not the way it was when I was growing up. I guess it wasn't permanent then either, because I was always growing up, whether I realized it or not, but now I do realize it, and everything has changed.

You can't "un-know" something, can you? Once you know something, you can never return to the state of not knowing it. Unless you run your car into a tree and wind up with amnesia. But seriously, I couldn't be a little girl now, even if I wanted to, because I know things I didn't know when I was a little girl, and my little-girlness depended on me not knowing them. In some ways, this is good. I know much more about being a person and about living in the world. But I feel like I've lost something, too. I've lost time, if nothing else, days of my life that have gone by and won't return.

Sigh. Time to stop depressing myself with too much introspection. I think I'll go eat Greek cookies and try out whether I can make Eleni tell me the whole story of her life by talking to her incessantly until bedtime.

Will I still write to you now that I'm at college, Saint Lydia? I brought you with me, but will I keep you, or will you be something that slips away from me, too?

I don't know.

I would miss you. I don't think that has changed.

Love,

Lydia

Dear Lydia,

I join in your laughter over this amazing coincidence! But you must know, dear girl, that there is nothing in creation that is actually "random," as you call it. Certainly, God has a sense of humor, but He has given you and Eleni to one another for a definite purpose.

Eleni is a darling girl, just as you are, and it is a joy to hear of this new friendship. I pray that it will be a lifelong source of delight and fruitfulness to you both.

I see that already, one of your burdens has fallen away. You now have someone in whom to confide. You have someone to talk to whom you can see, as you were hoping.

I must tell you a secret about feeling happy and sad at the same time. Listen to me, Lydia, because this is important.

Pain exists because of beauty, and beauty exists because of pain. If there were nothing beautiful in creation, we would feel no pain, because we would not know the meaning of loss. And yet, the pain is itself an acknowledgment of beauty and a reminder of our need to return to it. If we could not suffer, it would be because we had nothing worth suffering for. It would be a creation tasting only of sawdust and ashes. God gives us beauty to lift us out of pain and pain to return us to beauty. It is a cycle of the spirit, as rain and rivers and evaporation are a cycle of the earth.

Write to me now that you are in college, Lydia. Write to me often and speak to me truthfully. Let me be part of the beauty in your life, and in temptation, let me be part of the pain that brings you back to life.

In prayer and with great love,
Saint Lydia

September 3

Dear Saint Lydia,

Whoooooohoooooooooooooooooo! I love being in college! Everything is going to be perfect because I made it onto the yearbook staff! *Really! I did!* This is unbelievably great. We make the yearbook, and we go to all these seminars on photography, layout, publishing, and photojournalism, so it even counts as a for-credit course. Not only that, everyone on earth knows that if you're on the yearbook staff, you're automatically cool. You're on a mission with an expensive camera, and the whole school's trying to get in your pictures. You are to undergraduates what café society is to fast food. Time to wear black and start blogging. You've made it!

College almost doesn't seem like "school" now because I'm doing something that is so amazing here. How often do you have to be responsible for something you *wanted to do anyway*?

Giddy! That's what I am!

It was just plain *fun* today. We went out in teams to photograph the first day of classes. We each took a camera and shot hundreds of pictures of everything we saw. Our faculty advisor told us to look for things that will seem characteristic of the "first day of school," and to look for "human-interest stories," which means images of funny or interesting events that will draw people into the picture and make them want to know the story behind it. He said to dig into the scene and take intimate, accurate pictures, but he reminded us to include some feel-good shots that will make good memories when we look at our yearbooks 50 years from now. What on earth will I think of college 50 years from now? Will I even care? How could I not care? But won't I have something more important than this to think about by then?

I'm off to play with my camera and learn what all the buttons and programming will make it do.

Love,

Lydia

P.S. I wish I could take a picture of you. I wish I could point my camera at thin air and then discover your face in the picture, magically detected by the camera's eye.

Dear Lydia,

Congratulations on this achievement, and please accept my best wishes for a year of adventurous learning and delight!

We did not have cameras in my day, but the idea of looking for "pictures" among your fellow humanity is intriguing. No doubt you will soon train your eye to see what it has not seen before. You have spent so much time trying to find meaning in the words you hear. Perhaps now you will find another outlet for your questing spirit and learn to see meaning in pictures.

In some sense, you are embarking on the task of iconography, of making the truth you see around you apparent in a visual representation. You are attempting to capture motion in stillness, life in art. It seems there is a language or method to photography just as there is to iconography. In iconography, certain objects or events are always depicted in certain ways so that they will be readily understood by centuries of observers far removed from the originals. These methods are also used to draw the observer away from the natural plane of the picture to the spiritual plane of what it is intended to convey. This is why we call icons "windows into heaven." One should look through an icon, not at it. Might this sometimes be true of photography, I wonder? When you speak of a "human-interest" picture, I think perhaps you mean a picture in which the observer's mind moves beyond the actual depiction and conjures what is not visible in the picture, the sounds and feelings, the rest of the story, its meaning.

As to taking a photograph of me, you do not need to, dear girl. You told me in the first letter you ever wrote to me that you have an icon of me. Keep looking at it. I am there.

In Christ our Icon and our Light,
Saint Lydia

21

September 19

Dear Saint Lydia,

So, let me fill you in on my life here.

Our campus is on the west side of a town that isn't much bigger than the campus. The campus could be a town of its own. All the freshmen women live in one dorm, but Maria Louisa, Jill, Lauren, and I are all on different floors. They each have a new roommate, just like I do, and I guess we're all busy getting used to our new life. We see each other at volleyball practice, and sometimes in the dining hall, but that's about it! Volleyball here is harder and more time-consuming than it was in high school. I still love to play, but college sports seem to be a lot more intense and competitive than high school sports were. Sometimes it's hard to remember that it's just a game.

My roommate Eleni is the best. If I believed in reincarnation, I would say we had already been friends in three or four lifetimes before this one. We can talk to each other about anything, we make each other laugh hysterically, and we both seem to want the same things out of life.

Rooming with her is perfect. We rearranged all the furniture and put up curtains and posters and a little potted plant we hope we don't kill with neglect. We even found a dead bug in our ceiling light and named him Rigor Mortis so we could have a pet. Every night, we hang out in our pajamas taking twice as long to do our homework because we're talking constantly. We had to make a rule that we would work for twenty minutes and talk for five. That was because one night we accidentally stayed up till 3:00 AM just *talking*. I'm in heaven.

Eleni uses air freshener that smells like incense (she says she can't be Orthodox and live in a room that doesn't ever smell like incense), and the girl down the hall came in and started laughing and asking what she had been smoking in here that she had to cover up. Eleni made this snorting derogatory noise . . . I really can't spell it, but it's soooooo effective at shutting people up . . . and said, "You're such a freak, Pogo. Incense was around way before druggies started using it to cover their sins. Don't you even know what it's for?" Pogo looked stupid for a minute, and then Eleni took pity on her and said it was to keep us in touch with holy things. Pogo's mouth fell open, but the crazy thing about Eleni is that she's so confident in who she is that people just can't embarrass her. She never wavered. It was Pogo who was stupid, not Eleni, and Eleni was so sure of this that Pogo believed her.

I forgot you don't know who Pogo is. She says that name came from some joke that happened at a party she went to in high school, and now she's so used to being called Pogo that it weirds her out when people call her Emmeline. Eleni says she should have more self-respect than that, but I can kind of see why she wouldn't want to be Emmeline.

Pogo is a funny creature. She has the best intentions in life, but she never seems to have it all together about anything. She's insanely good at math. She can do differential equations in her head while she brushes her teeth. But it's like all her smartness got used up in one place. Math is all she can do. Her clothes usually don't match. Her hair always looks like she slept on it. She gets drunk at Fraternity Row almost every weekend (and did I mention we are still underage?), and if she can't remember how to call the safety shuttle to get back to the dorm, she just calls whatever number she can remember until someone answers. Last weekend, she called the math department office and left a very irate message on their answering machine in the middle of the night because she thought she had called the safety shuttle and no one was answering. They gave her *so* much grief on Monday morning. Probably she will invent a revolutionary computer programming language or save the world in some other way, unless she accidentally walks in front of a freight train and dies young.

Okay, I *really* need to do homework. My hardest class is English. You wouldn't think that would be hard. Just reading books and writing about them, right? Wrong. We have to basically psychoanalyze every book we read. We have to pick all the characters apart, including the author, who is somehow now a character, and make up all this deep meaning out of the text which, frankly, I'm not sure is even there. But this professor thinks psychology is the answer to everything. When I get out of that class, I think my own life is an exercise in psychology. Eleni says he was probably dropped on his head as a child and never recovered.

Love,

Lydia

Dear Lydia,

Eleni has great sense! Pogo is living up to her name. She must become Emmeline again. She has allowed herself to be defined by a rude jest. Think what she has done, Lydia! She has made herself complicit with this rudeness.

She has told herself that it is acceptable for her to be treated badly, and not only does she allow others to mistreat her, but she has begun to mistreat herself. She is created in the image of God! How can she permit such an abuse? She has given up her name! No wonder she is scattered and broken.

Look at the contrast between Pogo and Eleni. Eleni, as you have said, is so confident in who she is that others take her at her own estimation of herself. She believes what she says, and her belief is contagious. Of course she cannot be embarrassed! What has she to be ashamed of? Eleni knows who created her, and she has confidence in His skill.

You must never give yourself up to evildoers, dear girl. You must never allow them the malicious victory of turning you against yourself. If you begin to attack yourself and believe in the destruction of your own value, you are lost, and you have empowered your enemy beyond his wildest dreams. He will go out to seek new victims on the strength of your encouragement. You must never allow this, Lydia. Never.

Your professor's confidence in psychology may have the same corrosive effect. I have seen his kind before. He is one of those who must have all truth in human terms. He wishes to recreate creation in the image of man because he cannot accept that it has already been created in the image of God. Poor fellow. His creation is a house of cards, and it will collapse under the first sustained force that strikes it.

Psychology in its rightful mind is the productive study of the human psyche and its workings in the assorted contexts of creation. A real student of the subject is more interested in learning what there is to know than in adjusting his learning to suit his own insecurities.

But I grow too harsh. One must struggle to keep mercy in one's judgment and to remember that God is fully capable of protecting His own without relying on our indignation.

In Christ the Omnipotent,
Saint Lydia

October 6

Dear Saint Lydia,

Remember I told you that Paul was coming here on a science scholarship? Today I took a photograph of his biology lab for yearbook, and it was the strangest experience of my college life so far (all eight weeks of it, but seriously, it was unique).

We were taking pictures of students during classes today. We had permission to go in any classroom and take photographs, provided we didn't disrupt the class or disturb the students in any way. My teammate today was Pearse, who's a sophomore from yearbook, and he's really shy, so I always do the talking for both of us, but he takes good pictures. So Pearse and I went into one of the science classrooms to take pictures of students in a cellular biology lab. I personally have no idea what cellular biology is, meaning I don't know why it's called cellular and how it's different from plain old biology, which about killed me my freshman year of high school. On assignment for yearbook is the only way I'll ever be in an advanced science lab. I just don't have that kind of brain.

Pearse found something he wanted to photograph near the back of the room, so I just tiptoed around on my own. Frankly, I might have felt shy myself, except I've discovered that you can hide behind a camera. Not literally, but when you have one, you can focus your attention completely on the camera without anyone expecting you to do anything else, and you can also bet that most people around you are focused more on the camera than they are on you. They're wondering whether you're taking a picture of them and whether their hair looks good or if the big zit on their nose is showing. My hair and nose aren't under scrutiny because I'm the one holding the camera. It makes me unselfconscious, and I'm sure I get better pictures and more of them because of this.

So me and my freedom-making camera were going the rounds, and I was just bringing a shot into focus when I heard a voice beside me saying, "You're missing the best stuff. Take a picture of this. It's the most beautiful thing in here." I was startled. I paused and then lost the shot I was about to take because the people moved away. I turned to see who was talking to me, feeling pretty annoyed, and it was Paul!

I think this may be the first three sentences he ever spoke to me. Not to me as a classmate participating in the same teacher-guided discussion. Words spoken only to me, for me. I just stood there, and I hope my mouth wasn't hanging open, but he wasn't looking at me. He was focusing this little projector that was hooked up to the special microscope he was using so that he could project the image from the microscope onto the wall beside his lab table. He flicked his little button, and poof! An image came up on the wall. It was amber-colored and incredibly intricate, and I couldn't identify what it was. I turned my head toward him, and he said, "Fern spore case."

I remember fern spore cases. At least, I think that's what they were.

We had to dig up the right type of fern in the woods somewhere, keep it alive until we got to class, and then slice it up all kinds of ways to make slides of different parts. What a nightmare. But I didn't remember anything like this, so I said, "I've seen a fern spore case, but it didn't look like that!" And he said, "Yes, it did. You just needed a more powerful lens." And he smiled at me, a little secret smile, like he knew his lens was better than mine was, but maybe also like he knew I could see the difference, like he could.

The image was beautiful. I took five pictures of it, trying out the little camera tricks I've learned until I got a clear picture of all those tiny, tiny parts that no one would ever have seen at all without the invention of microscopes. But they were there just the same, whether we could see them or not.

We were only in the classroom for about ten minutes, and the fern spore case epiphany only lasted for five, but I couldn't shake the feeling that something had *happened*. I don't mean "Wow, Paul and I had a moment, maybe he'll ask me out." I don't think he goes out with girls who need a more powerful lens. I mean something happened to *me*. I got close to something big, some big idea about much more than fern spore cases.

It was the idea that the reality of "invisible" things has nothing to do with my ability to see them. And then the idea that I can see them clearly if only I have the right lens, the lens with high enough power.

Maybe I could see you if I had the right lens, Saint Lydia. Maybe I could see God.

All shaken up,
Lydia

Dear Lydia,

Glory to God for all things!

You have got the door open, dear girl. You have got hold of the knob and wrenched it open just a crack. Pull harder, dear girl, pull harder!

Yes, yes! It is all there! Its reality has nothing to do with your ability to see it. You could see it all clearly if only you had a more powerful "lens."

Beloved child, we are all here waiting, breathlessly, to be seen. The most Holy Trinity, your loving Creator, the dear Theotokos, the angels, the saints, your loved ones who have died, your own spiritual self and all the transcendent delight and satisfaction that could be yours, that is yours, if only you will find it and claim it.

Do not close the door again, Lydia. Keep it open and keep your face pressed to the crack until you gather your strength to fling it wide.

With all my love,

Saint Lydia

23

October 11

Dear Saint Lydia,

Here I am in the middle of the night again. I couldn't explain this to anyone else, but you are you, so I can tell you about it, I'm sure.

I was going to try to pray.

It all started with the fern spore case. (Wow. That sounds like the first line of a very bad novel.) Remember? The more powerful lens? I had such a strong feeling, like there was something right there, right next to me, if I could only figure out how to get to it. So tonight, I set the alarm on my watch because no one but me would hear it.

I fell asleep on my arm, staring at my watch, so it beeped right in my ear and woke me up at 2:00 AM. I picked that time because I was sure I would have it all to myself. I didn't turn on any lights. I just sat up in bed.

But then I wasn't sure what to do next. So I got on my knees and folded my hands and closed my eyes . . . *and totally freaked myself out.*

I don't know what happened to me, Saint Lydia. I don't know if I just felt so self-conscious I couldn't handle it and had to hide under the covers, or if it was more than that. I suddenly felt like I was playing with fire. If I was admitting there might actually be some point to praying, then I had to also admit there might be Someone there to pray to, Someone who might even answer me. I lost my nerve. It was like hanging up without even dialing a number. I couldn't open my mouth to start the conversation.

Since when did I ever have a spiritual feeling of any kind, let alone one that could get me up in the middle of the night? But it turned out to be nothing after all. I felt like I walked right up to the edge of a cliff in total confidence that God would hold me up, and then just as I was going to put out my foot to take the first step into thin air, all my confidence drained away, and I couldn't make myself keep believing there was any point to what I was going to do.

But even then, I wasn't sure if I stopped because of disbelief or because of cowardice or even some kind of mental laziness. When you come right down to it, even though it's often a big struggle and fills my life with turmoil, it's easy to be deciding about religion. It's hard to make a commitment.

So now I'm caught. I have one half of myself holding onto my doubts, to what is familiar, and the other half of me that genuinely wanted to step off the cliff. That other half of me really wants to know what would happen if I flung myself out into the air. Would I discover God, or would I discover another round of doubts and struggles? I wonder.

But I'm disgusted with myself because now I've realized that it's the easy way out to just keep on wondering.

Going back to bed, with a sigh,

Lydia

Dear Lydia,

I must make you acquainted with my friend Saint Peter, who once had a similar experience when riding in a fishing boat. He saw Jesus walking toward him on the water, and he was so eager to join Him that he stepped out of the boat and began walking to Jesus across the water. There he was, a stone's throw from God, doing what is not possible for any human being, but suddenly, his confidence deserted him and he began to sink. You may say, "Of course he sank!" but, you see, he had been walking successfully on the surface of the water until that moment when he stopped believing that he could.

You are there in your fishing boat, dear girl, and you must get out of it. I know you worked hard even to enter the boat, but now you must step out onto the water, and once you have done that, you must keep walking. You must see that the reality of Christ walking toward you is more powerful than the reality of the water beneath your feet.

It is the puzzle of living in the natural world. It seems so real. In fact, it seems to be all there is of reality. But this is an illusion. The supporters of the illusion are loud and long-winded, and they resent anyone who does not agree with them. For this reason, they are not worthy opponents. You would do better to ignore them and focus on the loving Figure moving toward you across the water. The water itself is only the means by which you can reach Him.

I will pray for you and for your desire to pray. Although you do not think of them as such, your letters to me are almost prayers themselves. Speaking to a saint is right next door to speaking to God. In both instances, you are acknowledging the reality you cannot see. But in the case of speaking to God, you are acknowledging Reality Itself.

Just keep trying, Lydia. You will succeed.

In Christ who walks on water,
Saint Lydia

24

October 13

Dear Saint Lydia,

My pictures of the fern spore case came out well. I experimented with colors when I printed them out, and I have one beautiful image in amber and another in black and white that shows the intricacy of the cells.

To commemorate his unknowing participation in my little epiphany, I sent copies of the pictures to Paul in campus mail, with a note. It said, "Dear Paul, Here are my photographs, in honor of the more powerful lens. Thank you, Lydia." I kept copies for myself as well. They are here between the pages of my journal.

Getting tape to attach them to a page,
Lydia

P.S. It's me again. I walked past the biology laboratory on my way back from volleyball practice this afternoon. I was meeting a friend near there so we could go to dinner together. The room was empty, but the lights were on, and I saw the photographs I sent Paul pinned up over his work-station in the laboratory. The scholarship students have their own tables in that room. How funny that my unscientific pictures are there. It just shows that there's more than one way to see, even through a microscope.

Dear Lydia,

I have noticed that God sometimes creates a moment that is like a little room, a separated place that does not partake of the time and space around it. It is a place in which something can be discovered, divided out of the obscurity so that it stands out in relief, visible by contrast but only to those inside the room. The room dissolves as quickly as it forms, but the effect survives its dissolution, and the occupants of the room are changed.

You have explained to me what meaning you took from your moment with Paul and his microscope. To date, you have not described him as a sympathetic person, or one likely to perceive or understand another person's experience, especially an experience as intangible as this. You did not say anything to him (at least, not that you have told me) that would have informed him that you found any special meaning in what he showed you.

Yet he chose to keep the photographs you sent him and to hang them up where he and others will see them often. Do you wonder why? What are the possible reasons? You may think he has displayed them as a testament to his own skill, to his expertise with a microscope. But it is just as likely that he found them exquisite, as you did, and that he is not so devoid of human understanding as you believe him to be. He is intelligent, in your estimation. He has sensibility—he told you himself that the cells under his microscope were beautiful. Beautiful. This is not the observation of cold science, dear girl.

You say truly that there is more than one way to see. Is it not possible that Paul sees more than you suspect?

> In prayer that you yourself will learn more than one way of seeing,
> Saint Lydia

25

Dear Saint Lydia,

Today in yearbook, I was sorting some papers for the files we have to keep for our faculty advisor. I was using a big table near the back of the yearbook room, and Lauren and Jill came in when they saw me through the open door. They were talking a mile a minute because Jill's parents are getting a divorce. Out of the clear blue sky. Lauren found out this past weekend when she went home with Jill over Saturday, so now Jill is telling everyone. It's hard to know how Jill is taking this. She's the funny girl, and she can laugh even at this, at her own home life falling apart. Lauren was being supportive, agreeing with whatever Jill said, obviously trying to show her that her "volleyball family" is still as strong as ever, no matter how crazy her real family has gone.

Apparently, the divorce has already happened, and Jill didn't tell anyone until now. This makes me wonder what's happening to our group of friends. We were so close last year. We had no secrets from each other. We didn't *want* any secrets from each other. But look at us now! Trella gets pregnant and loses her boyfriend, and we don't hear about it until she's forced to stay home from college. Jill's parents get a divorce and she says nothing until Lauren finds out for herself. What else don't I know? Who else is going through some major life event without telling me?

I was a little upset, but I decided not to show it. Jill has enough on her plate without worrying about my feelings. So Lauren and Jill sat with me while I finished my job, and we let Jill tell us as much as she wanted us to know. She said that now that her parents are divorced, their "lifestyles" are changing, and her mom is now Buddhist, but her dad is still Catholic like they always were. Lauren said, "Oh, so what does that make you?" And Jill said that she doesn't want to take sides, so she does Buddhist stuff with her mom and Catholic stuff with her dad. Fair enough. I can see that would be one way to solve the problem. But then Lauren said, "Yeah, but what are you really? Are you just faking one of them out?" Jill answered that actually, it's all good, because now she just takes whatever she likes about Buddhism and whatever she likes about Catholicism and puts it together to make her own personal religion. (Maria Louisa, the Super-Catholic, would have lost her mind at this point!) Then Jill went off about how it was so cool and so meaningful to have beliefs that she chose for herself, and Lauren was gushing with sympathy and support for Jill's new spiritual life.

Now, I realize that Jill's in a difficult position. Her parents went off in two directions, but she's still attached to both of them, so she has to do something to keep from being pulled apart. I hope they know what they're putting her through.

But—

Can you really do that? Can you really just take a slice from every plate and put it all in one plate and claim that makes it a pie? Buddhism doesn't even have the same God as Catholicism, so how on earth does that work? And if she just goes around picking out what she likes about everything, that means she can leave out all the hard parts!

So basically, she's worshipping something that she made up for herself. What kind of God would that be? How can it be God if *you* made it up? Isn't that right next door to worshipping yourself? And if it's just you underneath all that fancy talking, it isn't worth worshipping, is it? Whatever this is that you made up is just that—it's *made up*. It never did anything for anybody. It isn't *true*. That means that something else *is* true, and *you* don't know what it is because you're too busy playing with this religion toy that you made for yourself.

What good is that?

It's like being a kid, playing Buzz Lightyear, and jumping off the deck yelling, "To infinity and beyond!" Well, you can tell yourself you are Buzz, but your neck is going to be just as broken when you hit the turf.

People are cuckoobirds. I'm going to see if there's any chocolate around this place.

Love,

Lydia

Dear Lydia,

A cuckoo bird would never do anything so irrational as concocting an imaginary god for itself. One must hope that after eating some chocolate, you will see how greatly you have wronged the animal kingdom. To be sure, they have no reasoning powers in the human sense, but nor do they create alternative realities to avoid dealing with what troubles them.

You do not seem to realize that you yourself are going through a "major life event" without confiding in your friends. You have not mentioned "The Religious Situation" to any of them. You did not tell them of your family's conversion or of your spiritual struggles and explorations. You did not even invite them to your birthday party because you did not want to explain the fasting food your family would be eating. You invited them last year. You have changed as much as they have. Your friendship with this "volleyball family" will only outlast your time on the volleyball team if you begin to explore your relationships in more mature contexts. As you face greater challenges and complexities in your life, some of these friendships will fade because they are not substantial enough to withstand the pressures of adult life. But some will grow stronger and brighter, like precious metal rising from the refiner's fire.

Jill is in a difficult circumstance, as you have noted, and sadly, her parents have set her adrift instead of guiding her through it. I am glad to see you show her mercy (however temporarily) because she is bearing a burden that is not of her own making.

That being said, I must now agree wholeheartedly with the rest of your sentiments. You are quite right that a "made-up" God is no God at all, and like you, I cannot imagine how one could construct a single deity out of the combination of Buddhism and Catholicism.

I am not acquainted with Buzz Lightyear himself, but I am well aware of the human propensity for replacing unpleasant fact with appealing fiction. People have an almost limitless ability to pretend things to themselves and to close their eyes tightly against the total inability of these inner pretenses to direct the world outside, the world that is not within their control.

It is all fear of death, Lydia. They scramble about trying to control the world around them because somewhere deep in their souls, they are hoping to prevent their own death. If only they knew that they need not worry. Someone Else has already saved them from death. To be sure, we each encounter a physical death of some kind, but this should not frighten us if we realize that it is only a door and that further and better life awaits us on the other side of it.

In Christ who trampled down death,
Saint Lydia

October 22

Dear Saint Lydia,

Pogo is sleeping with us tonight because her roommate's boyfriend is coming over to spend the night in their room. Pogo says her roommate bought all this food to make a romantic dinner for two and then a romantic breakfast for two, and you can bet your bed socks they aren't going to spend the time between those two meals playing Monopoly.

I realize this is carrying talking about boys to a saint right out to the limit, but when Pogo showed up at our door with her pillow and a quilt, we all started talking at once, and later, Eleni brought you into it, so now I have to tell you the whole story because Eleni is sure you'll have an opinion.

(I should tell you that I told Eleni all about you. I even told her about that dream I had that you were writing back to me, and Eleni said, "Well, of *course* she's writing back to you! It's too bad you psyched yourself out and didn't get to read the letters. I wish a saint would write *me* letters.")

First of all, it's totally against dorm rules to have a man in your room overnight. So if the RA (the dorm assistant in charge of our floor) catches Pogo's roommate, she will be in serious trouble. Obviously, she doesn't care. And furthermore, this isn't fair to Pogo! She *clearly* can't stay in the room with the two lovebirds in there, and it's her room too, so she has more right to be there than the boyfriend does. But if Pogo's not going to stand up for herself, I guess we can't do it for her.

So Pogo made herself comfortable (we each gave her an extra pillow because this floor is concrete and a quilt's not going to be enough), shamelessly passed on all the gossip she knows about her roommate and the boyfriend, and asked us to turn on the TV. We were hoping to get some rest, but we're nice. We turned it on and found a boringly generic chick-flick that put her to sleep in about fifteen minutes.

After Pogo fell asleep, Eleni leaned over and started whispering to me. "Pogo has no control of her life at all," she hissed. "Does she realize she just got thrown out of her own room?! Who lets that happen?" Then she flopped back on her pillow and asked what on earth Saint Lydia would say to it all. I said, "I have no idea, but if Pogo makes a habit of moving in here, I'm going to have something to say about it!" Eleni laughed at me and said, "I'm sure Saint Lydia would be more upset with Pogo's sexy roommate. Well, no, she'd probably say Pogo was aiding and abetting them. But to be fair to Pogo, I'm sure most people would do what she did. I'm a crazy-woman. I would have stood on the bed and bawled them out. They would have been glad to sleep under a park bench when I got through with them."

Eleni's right, of course. It's definitely not cool to interfere with somebody else's sex life. You might as well hang a sign around your neck that says "Prude," because if you get mad at someone for having sex (even in *your* room!), everyone assumes you aren't getting any yourself. And if that's what they think of you, you cease to exist in the social world. I don't know of even three people who admit to being virgins. Probably some people are claiming more sex than they're actually having, but nobody's walking around proud of having *none*. Your parents tell you that the big deal is doing it at all, but when you get out into the world, you discover that nobody cares if you're doing it but only how you're doing it and with whom. There's even a saying here that the day a virgin graduates, the two stone statues by the east gate will get down off their pedestals and dance.

Everyone is sleeping with someone. Everyone except the geeks, Eleni, and me. Well, that's probably an exaggeration, but that's how it *feels*, and I have to wonder sometimes why we don't. It's not that we're unattractive. I don't mean to sound vain. I'm just being realistic. We aren't virgins because we don't have a choice. So why are we? What's the deep-down real reason? Are we not having sex because we have strong beliefs or just because we haven't met anyone who really attracts us yet? Will I still stick to what my mom taught me when I have a mad crush on a grown man who's ready, willing, and able?

I'm not trying to be disrespectful to you, Saint Lydia. Who else but you can I talk to about this, except maybe Eleni? Remember what happened when I tried to tell my mom about Trella? Imagine what she would say to all this going on right in the same dorm with me!

Pogo is snoring. Great. I'm going to get no sleep tonight. Thanks a lot, Pogo's roommate.

Love,
Lydia

Dear Lydia,

I do not feel disrespected, dear girl. I am always happy when you confide in me, no matter what subject you wish to discuss.

Poor Pogo! She seems to go from one misfortune to the next. It is chaos breeding chaos, I suppose. I agree that Pogo should stand up for herself, but she has already given away her name, so it does not surprise me that she is now giving away her room. She cannot prevent her roommate's disorderly behavior, but she can demand that it not take place in her own living space. Perhaps she made the attempt and her roommate refused to listen to her. In that case, she could have appealed to a higher authority.

It always saddens me to learn of any couple's decision to engage in marital intimacy outside the bonds of marriage. I am sure your mother has taught you that this is expressly forbidden by the Church. In fact, the Orthodox are not alone in forbidding premarital sex, as you call it. (This term seems misleading because it means "before marriage," and in most cases, no marriage is planned or intended!) To my knowledge, all the major Christian faith groups share a belief that sexuality was created to physically express spiritual love that has been consecrated before God in the marriage sacrament, and to provide for the procreation of children.

But even supposing that you do not share these beliefs, and I think it is safe to say that Pogo's roommate does not, sex without marriage is still unwise. Too often, it happens for the wrong reasons and ends in bitter disillusionment for one or both participants. There are also physical risks, the risk of contracting one of many painful and dangerous diseases and the risk of conceiving a child that one or both of you is unable or unwilling to parent. (For example, Trella is unable to raise her child without help from her parents, and Chad appears to be unwilling to raise the child at all.)

Heartbreak is the most common aftermath, and I will tell you why.

God created human sexuality as the fruit of a deeply committed spiritual love. He designed it to be a completion, a giving of the whole of oneself to the one who is loved. Because this is its purpose, it is in the nature of sexual intercourse to open the lovers to one another, causing a degree of vulnerability that is safe only inside a marriage in which both parties are pledged to work together in the growth and enjoyment of their love.

Without this commitment, the vulnerability is dangerous. It is like a cut in the skin. A surgeon may cut into your skin to reach some organ that requires care and healing. A surgeon's incision is like vulnerability in marriage; it serves a useful purpose and occurs only in an environment that is safe and clean. But vulnerability outside of marriage is like a wound sustained in an accident, like cutting yourself on a sharp rock or by falling from a cliff. It lays the victim open to infection and pain, and it can bleed uncontrollably, draining life away.

I will pray for you and Eleni that you will abstain from the dangers you see all around you. It is my hope that you will find strength in yourselves, and that will come only when your decisions are based on your own beliefs, not simply on your mothers' teaching. In the adult world, you can no longer refer back to parental authority. You must make your own faith the authority you turn to for permission or for the power to resist.

In Christ our enduring strength,
Saint Lydia

27

October 23

Dear Saint Lydia,

This morning, I walked into the bathroom on our hallway to brush my teeth, and there was the boyfriend, the guy who spent the night with Pogo's roommate. He was standing there in nothing but his boxer shorts, brushing his teeth in *our* bathroom. This is a women's dorm, and this is most definitely a women's bathroom. There's a sign on the door that says "Women." He doesn't look illiterate.

He was quite friendly. He chatted away like he'd known me forever. I thought of several extremely rude things I could say to him, but instead, I just brushed my teeth and went back to my room. Does this make me polite or cowardly?

It's not that I'm a prude. I really don't think I am. For better or worse, sex is beginning to seem a little commonplace to me. I hear about it all the time. I'm getting numb. But it made me angry that he would come in our bathroom. He's not *my* boyfriend. How does she know the rest of us want to see him in his underwear, let alone wanting him to see us in ours?

Eleni spilled pink, scented lotion all over his towel while he was in the shower. *Not* by accident. I wish I could think as fast as she can.

All morning, I've been wondering about something I said to you last night. I said that if Pogo wouldn't stand up for herself, we couldn't do it for her. Is this true?

As I was standing there in the bathroom, it struck me that because I have now witnessed the presence of the boyfriend with my own eyes, I have evidence. I could call the RA and tattle to her about Pogo's roommate. The RA is at the far end of our floor, but she could probably get here before he got his clothes on or his stuff hidden.

I didn't do it. I didn't even tell Eleni I thought about it. Eleni seems to think the lotion got the message across.

It's the difference between vigilante justice and calling on the law. Everyone else on the hall thinks Eleni's lotion attack was hysterical. But if I told the RA and word got around that I had done it, I wouldn't have a friend at college within a week. Why is that? We all know what the rules are, so why would I be a pariah for following them?

But that's not my real question. My real question is whether I'm morally obligated to turn Pogo's roommate in. Is Pogo? Is Eleni?

And here's an even bigger problem. I happen to know that the reason our whole hallway smells *violently* of lavender potpourri every Sunday is because the girls in the room next to Pogo's smoke marijuana (and who knows what else) every weekend, and then they spray the whole room with air freshener afterwards because they think that hides the smell. They use so much air freshener that you can almost *see* the scented cloud floating down the hall. I don't know who they think they're fooling, but the point is that so far, they haven't gotten caught because they only do it in their own room and none of us has turned them in.

Drug use is against the law anywhere, not just on campus. So are we obligated to turn those girls in if we suspect them? Is it my job to bust into their room on Saturday night with a camera or to call the police to come over when I know they're in there smoking weed?

I have the uncomfortable feeling that it *is* my job, but I have the even more uncomfortable feeling that I don't have the courage to do it. It's not that everyone on my hall is a druggie. But I bet none of them has ever ratted on anyone, or if they have, they made sure no one knew about it.

What should I do?

As usual, I'm doing nothing because I'm not sure what to do. It feels *so awkward* to turn someone in that it's hard to believe it's actually the right thing to do. Maybe it's not the right thing to do. Maybe minding my own business about anything that's not happening in my own room is the right thing to do. I can't go around telling everyone how to live their lives and turning them in whenever they don't do what I say, can I? No, obviously not. But is turning in someone who's breaking the law two doors down from me the same as telling everyone how to live? Probably not.

I know I'm not going to do anything about this.

But I still want to know if this is a failure on my part or a sign of sanity.

Sigh.

Lydia

Dear Lydia,

When you are struggling to make a decision, it sometimes helps to turn the situation around in your mind and look at it from several angles.

I will give you two questions to answer that may help you consider the boyfriend situation and the drug situation in a new light. Try to answer both questions for both situations.

1. What will be the results of my actions?

2. How will my actions affect the other people in the situation?

Let us consider Pogo's roommate and her boyfriend first. You have mentioned two courses of action for yourself: you can turn them in to the RA or you can say nothing. What will be the result of informing the RA that Pogo's roommate had a young man staying in her room? What will the RA do? What will Pogo's roommate do? What will the boyfriend do? What will Pogo do? What will Eleni do? And when all of these people have taken their actions, what reaction have you planned for yourself? It is likely that the effects of your actions will come back to you in some form.

When you have played through these scenes in your mind, try to determine how your actions will affect each person involved. How will Pogo feel if you turn in her roommate? How will she feel if you do not turn in her roommate? Will someone else turn her in, or will Pogo be spending many weekends in your room because she cannot sleep in her own? Are you prepared to keep hosting her? How many times will Pogo stay in your room before you decide the situation has gone too far? Will it become more or less difficult to report the situation to the RA as time passes?

What message is being sent to Pogo's roommate if everyone knows her boyfriend is there and nobody turns her in? If he is using a public bathroom on your hall, she must realize that his presence is known. Clearly, she and her boyfriend expect you all to keep their secret. If you do not keep it, how will it affect them? If you do keep it, how will it affect them? How will it affect you?

Some might argue that illegal drug use is a more serious offense than the one Pogo's roommate is committing, but I cannot agree with them. However, I am aware that in your world, offenses against civil law are given precedence over offenses against spiritual law.

Again, you must ask yourself about the results and the personal effects of your actions. If you call the police, what will happen? What will the police do? What will the offenders do if they are caught? What will they do if they are not caught? What will happen to all of you if someone who does not live on your hall discovers the problem and calls the police?

Do the girls who are using the drugs know that their hallmates suspect them of drug use? Are they also, like Pogo's roommate, depending on all of you to keep their secret? Ask yourself about the effects on all of you and on them if you keep the secret.

Although I cannot support you in condoning wrongful and dangerous behavior, I am fully aware of the fearful challenge of upholding personal beliefs among people who do not share them and may actively condemn them. Your hesitation to attempt controlling the behavior of others is healthy, and it will save you and your loved ones much grief in life. But your fear that you do not have sufficient courage to act on your convictions saddens me. It may well be true that you lack courage, but it may also be that you do not know your own strength. You are newly entered into the adult world. You have not yet had much opportunity to wield the sword of your faith, and you do not know what to expect, even from yourself.

Pray. Seek God's will. And when He shows you His will, trust Him to give you the courage and stamina necessary to act on it.

> In Christ our Patient Shepherd,
> Saint Lydia

November 6

Dear Saint Lydia,

I went to Trella's house today. I wanted to see her. I haven't called her as often as I meant to, and she seems to be letting her old friendships go. She lives about 20 minutes from my parents' house, so going there took just about as much time as going all the way home. I rode a Greyhound bus from the terminal near campus, and I ate breakfast and dinner out of a bag, on the bus. I got a taxi from the bus station in Trella's town to her house. It was a long day.

Her mom was home, but after saying hello to me kind of awkwardly, she drifted away and left us to talk by ourselves. We sat on a blue over-stuffed sofa in their tasteful living room. The room made me feel like I should have worn makeup. I suddenly couldn't imagine how I had the nerve to think I could throw a baby shower for Trella. In this atmosphere, any party would fall flat.

Trella was awkward, too, at first, and that made me feel awkward, and for a few minutes, I thought it was a mistake to come. She looked so different that it was hard not to stare at her. It's not that her belly is very big yet, but it has started to show, and something about her whole body has changed. She's wearing maternity clothes, she has bigger breasts than she ever did as a teenage athlete, and she has shadows under her eyes. She was so confident and outgoing before, and now she's quieter and daydreams a little. She keeps at least one of her hands on her belly all the time, as if she's already holding her baby.

She asked me about volleyball, so I told her everything I could think of about the team and what all the girls are up to these days. Then I stopped and said, "Trella, I'm just making you sad. I didn't come here to make you sad." She said, "You're not making me sad. I miss all of you, but I want to miss you. I don't want to let go of it. If all I can have is second-hand stories, then at least let me have that!"

I wanted to tell her she could have more than that, but I can't speak for the other girls. Lauren and Jill don't talk about her much any more, and I'm not really in touch with the girls who went to other colleges. I know Trella's still close with Maria Louisa, but I don't want to get her hopes up about the rest of them. So I just told her "secondhand stories."

Then I asked her about her life. She said she's tired, but the morning sickness is mostly over now, as long as she eats little snack meals all day long. "I think a lot," she said, after we sat there quietly for a few minutes. "I think about how I got here, and I think about Chad and why he left, but mostly, I think about my baby and what I want life to be like for her or him, and what I can do to make it that way, since I decided to raise my baby myself." She picked up a pencil on the coffee table and started twiddling with it. I wish I was like Maria Louisa and could put my arms around her spontaneously. I wish I knew if that was the right thing to do. I tried to think my good will for her so strongly that it would radiate out of me and she would feel it. She said, "This is going to be really hard, Lydia. How can I be a mother in my own mother's house?"

There were tears in her eyes. I had no wisdom for her, so I sat on the sofa with her as long as I could without missing the bus. Then I called a cab because her mom had gone out and taken the car. At the door, Trella reached out her hand and we shared a quick, awkward hug.

On the way home in the bus, I thought about love. I love Trella. Chad didn't love Trella, or if he did, he didn't love her enough. Trella loves her mom, but I think she loves her baby more. I think Trella's mom loves Trella, too. But I think her mom isn't much better at showing Trella love than I was. Maybe my mom would be like that, too, if I were Trella. But I don't know. Seeing Trella's mom gives me a little perspective on my own fights with my mom. At least we've never had anything this big to fight over!

I still want Trella to have a baby shower. Maybe her relatives are planning one, but somehow I doubt it. I think our old teammates would come, but I'm not as sure about that as I was this summer when this all first happened. It almost seems like it would be better to have no baby shower than to have one that only a few people attended. I don't want my gesture of support to turn into proof of how many people have deserted her. Maybe Maria Louisa will have some good advice for me. Or Eleni. Eleni doesn't know Trella, but she's good at practical advice.

Lost in thought,
Lydia

Dear Lydia,

If you let her, Trella may become a closer friend to you now. I think the "daydreaming" quality you saw in her today is the effect of deep and constant reflection. There is much she should be working out for herself. It is good that she is planning her baby's life. She is learning to think ahead, and this can be a protection against falling into flawed decisions made in haste and without the benefit of thoughtful judgment. You may find that your own spiritual journeying has something in common with Trella's. Your circumstances are different, but you are both searching for your own faith and striving to build up your own inner life.

Seek Maria Louisa's counsel about the baby shower. It is a kind and loving thought, but you are wise to consider whether you will be able to execute it as well as you would hope. You may be able to find some more personal way of celebrating the baby and giving a gift, without laying Trella open to the risk of unkindness from others, intentional or otherwise.

I am glad to see that you are developing an instinct about your friends that leads you to pick the right person for the right time. From what you have told me, neither Lauren nor Jill would be a good advisor to you at this moment. Lauren supports indiscriminately, without considering what evil she may be enabling, and Jill has not learned to confront problems honestly. But you seem to know that and to seek out the friend who is wiser when you are in need of wisdom. In time, you will discover patterns in your dealings with your friends, and the patterns of meaningful interaction will show you the friendships that are growing and moving with you on your journey.

Love is a subject well worth pondering. No matter how much you learn about love, you will never know everything about it because its source is God, the Infinite and Eternal. It is good to see your own relationships in the context of other people's, as long as you do not use this comparison as an unhealthy habit to bolster insecurity or pride. But there is no harm in appreciating the good qualities in your loved ones when you notice them suddenly, by contrast.

I know you are dissatisfied with your response to Trella's sadness. You feel that you should have said more or acted more definitely for her good. But your presence is the strongest statement you could have made to her, and it comforted her more than any wise words or eloquent gesture could have done.

Wishing you grace and peace,
Saint Lydia

29

November 25

Dear Saint Lydia,

I'm home. It's Thanksgiving break, and I'm back in my own house again for the first time since I left for college. In a way, I feel like I'm back for the first time since my family converted, because we're having turkey today for Thanksgiving dinner, even though it's happening during the Nativity Fast, when they don't eat meat. My mom told me that she and Dad felt a little bad about my fasting birthday party, and they've realized it must be stressful for me to live with customs that affect me but have no meaning for me. So we're having turkey and all the trimmings, just like we used to before everything changed. Just for me.

So I wonder: Does this mean that tomorrow the fast is on again and I get to eat *all the leftovers myself?*

Just kidding. Mostly. It would be kind of mean to sit there gorging on turkey sandwiches while they're all eating rice and zucchini. My mom will probably make turkey soup and then freeze it without even tasting it. I won't taste it either. Remember what happened when I tried to eat cheese on a Wednesday? But it doesn't matter. Today, on Thanksgiving Day itself, all is right with my world.

I wish you could be here with me, Saint Lydia, just breathing in and out. The air smells good. It smells like turkey slowly roasting, and like apple pie cooling in the kitchen, and like poultry seasoning and butter-browned onions from my mom's stuffing recipe. Outside is cold and gray, inside is warm and gold. I love Thanksgiving Day. I want it to be exactly the same every year forever and ever.

Every year, we use the same dishes on the table, the same tablecloth, the same little Thanksgiving-only treats like figs and dates, and cranberry sauce that holds the shape of the can even after it's lying in the silver dish, and black olives piled in a silver bowl with a filigree handle on one side. And stuffing and potatoes and sweet potatoes and creamed onions and green beans with almonds and pie and pie and pie. And the cornucopia, which is a horn-shaped basket my mom puts out every year and fills with whatever fruit we choose, apples, oranges, grapes, pears, persimmons, pomegranates, star fruit, walnuts in the shell, whatever we like. Tirsa and I go fruit-crazy every year at the grocery store.

I spent the morning reading with Tirsa on the rug in her bedroom. Rilla kept us company, sitting on our feet and woofing happily when-ever we laughed. We read a "chapter book" together, taking turns read-ing (except Rilla, who can't) and making all the characters have different voices. Then Tirsa told me all the news from first grade and demonstrated her part as a member of the heavenly host in the Nativity play at church. She's the sweetest person in my family, the little icing rose perched on top of the sometimes lumpy cake. I've been thinking about the gifts in my life, trying to be grateful in honor of the day. I had breakfast early with Dad, made pies with Mom, and read on the rug with Tirsa, and these small things reminded me again that I love my whole family, even when they make me completely insane.

On another subject, I think there's something wrong about buying our "harvest" at the grocery store. Call me crazy, but it's a harvest feast. At some level, shouldn't we have picked all the food by hand in our own fields? Shouldn't we have gone out to get the turkey with an ax? Except that would be *disgusting*. The only way I can eat the turkey is if I *don't* have to go after it with an ax. I think this is what comes of keeping old rituals in modern life, and after all, there are some people out there who *did* raise the harvest, so they do the actual harvesting for all of us grocery-store farmers.

I'm going back to college in three days. Time always moves on, holidays come and go, and there I am, on to the next thing, willy nilly. I wonder what I'll be thankful for next year. Will I feel like Tirsa knows me as she's growing up at home without me around? Will I have solved The Religious Situation? Will I come home for Thanksgiving? Will it be just the same, the way it always is in my memories?

I'm going to sit in front of the warm stove with Tirsa. We can watch the turkey roasting in the oven and listen to the leaves blowing across the dry brown grass outside.

Love,

Lydia

Dear Lydia,

I am thankful for the compassion that moved your mother and father to celebrate this special day in the old way for your sake. Ritual is a human need. Even the smallest baby adores it. It is part of what makes Orthodox Christianity so lovable: it is full of ritual. The Divine Liturgy is like the waves of the sea, washing over us the same way, week after week, year after year. Certainly the Epistle and Gospel readings change, the saints are all commemorated in turn, the feast days come and go, but the Liturgy itself is the same, in prayer, in receiving the Eucharist, in rejoicing and going out in peace. And the feasts are rituals too, celebrations that come around every year and are commemorated in the same way each time, until they are as familiar as your own birthday and as happily anticipated.

God is always the same, and His Church is always the same. This does not present a problem because God is infinite and the Church is simply our meeting with Him. The Infinite is infinite. You may go on encountering God every day of your life without ever wearing Him out or coming to the end of His meaning. Indeed, coming daily to God is the only chance you have of getting to know Him at all. The ancient rituals of the Church do not suffer in translation to modern life because their Source is timeless. Their meaning was not dependent on their original context. The Holy Spirit can find us in whatever state of modernity we have contrived for ourselves. But unlike the "grocery-store farmers," believers cannot expect someone else to gather the spiritual harvest for them.

I think, dear girl, that you have discovered your sense of time passing. When you are a child, you have no sense of time. Even when you learn to tell the hours and the days and months, you do not yet understand that time passed has passed forever. Now you are on the brink of young womanhood, beginning your flight out of the nest, and you have realized that once you take this step, nothing is ever quite the same again. This is all in the order of things, but it is the end of childhood, and you are right to pause and cherish what you have had before you venture onward.

Do not fear, Lydia. Whatever you love deeply will never leave you. That is also in the order of things. Think how much depends on memory. It is a living gift of God.

In commemoration of all sacred memories,
Saint Lydia

30

November 27

Dear Saint Lydia,

Hello, it's me in the middle of the night. *Again.* Instead of trying to pray this time, I decided to just light a candle. I'm going back to college tomorrow, so I lit my candle tonight, while I'm still at home in a room by myself.

Candlelight always seems special to me. We light candles to celebrate things (I wonder why people do this . . . where did this tradition come from?), so maybe that's why, but I think there's something more to it than that. Hard to explain. So anyway, I lit a little scented candle on my window sill. It's a red pillar candle in a dimpled glass jar. Then I sat there on my bureau, next to the window, looking out at the dark night and then back at my little candle flame. Soon there was a clear pool of melted wax under the wick, and it smelled like roses.

I didn't do anything else. I just sat watching the candle burn, letting my thoughts wander freely. Sometimes I thought about you, sometimes I wondered about God, sometimes I thought about Eleni, and sometimes I thought about Maria Louisa telling me she doubts we could find enough people to come to a baby shower for Trella. That makes me sad, but she's probably right, so we aren't going to do it.

The candle is still lit, and I'm using its light to write to you, which seems appropriate . . . you lived so long ago, and now you're only present to me in my thoughts. It's a small flame, but I can feel its warmth on my face.

Being home again for the Thanksgiving holiday has reminded me of what I love here, but also of how I'm out of step with this little world. In some ways, I've grown a lot since I went away to college. In other ways, I think I'm standing still. I'm like a little boat with no wind in the sail, sitting on the water, waiting for a breeze. I'm waiting for something to come along and give me a push, I guess. I could tell you about it, but I've said it all before. I don't want to write you the same letter over and over again, chewing back and forth on my worries like Rilla chewing a bone until there's nothing left but shards on the ground and her teeth still anxious for more.

Look at me. I have now compared myself to a bone-mauling dog. When I lit this candle, I was having a quiet moment, trying to feel connected to something spiritual. And now I've reduced myself to a dog (no offense, Rilla, you're a great dog). Why can't I stay in that peaceful place? Why do my thoughts always tumble down?

It's winter. I can see cherry trees outside near the street light. The branches are bare now, but I know what kind of tree grows there, and I know the flowers will come in the spring.

Good night, Saint Lydia.

Love,

Lydia

Dear Lydia,

Your little candle is your faith, dear girl. It is a tiny flame, but you can already feel its warmth. I rejoice that you do whatever you can to keep it burning. If you cannot pray, at least you can be quiet and light a candle. It is a little act of worship, as you have rightly discerned. Trust your instinct about sacred things, Lydia. If something feels holy to you, draw near to it and test it. You will soon know whether it is of God.

I would not mind having the "same letter over and over again," but I can understand your weariness with all the familiar struggles. You are coming to a time of many changes in your life, and perhaps this will bring new perspectives and discoveries to freshen this still water on which you feel you are floating.

You ask why your thoughts always "tumble down." Ask instead what raises them to the heights from which they tumble. By what means are you able to discern and follow your impulse to worship quietly in the middle of the night? By what means are you able to feel the prick of disappointment when your sacred moment ends? How much in the presence of God are you already and do not know it?

Praying for your knowledge that the trees will blossom,
Saint Lydia

31

December 3

Dear Saint Lydia,

I'm back at school now. I'm wearing dark glasses and living on crackers and water at the moment. I can't believe I'm going to tell you about this, but I'm so used to talking to you that it seems like the natural response.

Eleni and I went to one of Pogo's parties last night, and we got so drunk we don't even remember what happened for most of it. I kind of remember some things, but I think I also had really vivid dreams all night, and I'm not sure which things actually happened and which things I dreamed.

It was a Fraternity Row party because one of Pogo's math geek friends is (weirdly enough) also a total frat boy. Pogo told us to wear old shoes because the floor would be inches deep in beer, and she was right. I should add that I can't stand being on the same side of the room as those shoes this morning because they smell so bad. The whole earth smells bad to me, and my head is going to explode if I have to move it more than one millimeter in any direction before tomorrow morning.

Eleni and I woke up at almost the same time this morning, and as soon as our eyes were unstuck and focused again, we both said, *"Never again!"* at the exact same time, as if we had planned it. Then Eleni threw up all over her bed, which almost made me throw up too. Actually, I think it would have, except that I have a vague feeling I already did throw up sometime last night. In some bushes, maybe? There are some strange scratches on my face that might have come from bushes. When we sat up, we found three girls we don't even know passed out on the floor of our room. We rolled them out into the hall. They were out cold. They mumbled a little, but they never woke up, and since they're all breathing just fine, I don't care if they sleep out there all day. Serves them right for going home with total strangers. Unless of course they helped us get home? What a fog I'm in.

I need some water, Saint Lydia. I'll write to you again when I feel better.

Love,
Lydia

Dear Lydia,

I am relieved to learn that you will go on speaking to me even when in such a deplorable condition as this. If you cannot keep from falling head-first over the obstacles placed daily in your path, at least it can be said for you that you do not commit the greater error of letting go of your only hope of getting up.

There is something important in this letter, as I consider it. I think you are telling me that you can see the chaos around you, the chaos of your own making. I rejoice that you recognize it for what it is.

Do not worry that I will pass judgment on you, dear girl. There is no one who lives who is without sin, and it is perhaps not surprising that you succumb to some of the many temptations thrust into your path in this larger world you are entering as you approach adulthood. I do not pass judgment on you or believe that this unfortunate decision to become intoxicated has harmed your spiritual future. But you must remember that you have only escaped great harm because you have rightly discerned that it was an error and seen clearly what rotten fruit it has borne.

Divine order is not unkind, but it is inevitable. God loves you as much when you fall as when you rise up, but His love does not extend to exempting you from the consequences of your misdeeds. Your body, for example, is created in such a way that when you misuse it, it becomes ill and makes you miserable. This does not mean that God does not love you; it means you have stepped outside of His order, outside the path to becoming a divine likeness. The cure is simple. You have but to step back in again. In this case, you have only to determine never to do it again, and the event will be closed, leaving no mark but that new knowledge from experience and the confirmation you receive by learning from it.

In prayer for your speedy recovery and renewed strength,
Saint Lydia

32

December 4

Dear Saint Lydia,

Hello again. Eleni and I are both feeling better, and since it's Saturday, we put our homework on hold and spent the evening just talking about last night and what happened.

Parties are crazy. I've only been to after-game parties with the volleyball team (and I've sneaked out to a few after-after-game-party parties), but Eleni has been "on the scene" at some wild ones. Some of her cousins live in New York City, and she spends part of her summers there. She said they always take her along to parties, but they're really strict with her and don't let guys hit on her or anything. It's because three of her cousins are guys themselves, and she says men are always protective of women in their own family because, being men, they know what men are like. I suggested that women do this for men too, but Eleni agreed only up to a point. She doesn't think most women think of men as needing protection. She said most of us just think they need *help*.

But anyhow, she says one party they went to was hosted by her oldest cousin's friend. This friend has a lot of money, and it was a huge party in a snazzy apartment, but the crazy part was that on the table with the pretzels and the chips and party peanuts was a dish of cocaine. *Cocaine.* It was just sitting there as if it was a dish of Goldfish crackers or something. Can you pass me some pretzels? Sure, can you pass me some cocaine?

The party we went to last night wasn't that bad. I mean, there wasn't any cocaine sitting out with the party peanuts. But for one thing, we are three years underage, so it was illegal for us to be drinking and for them to be serving alcohol to us and to more than half the people there (who were just as underage as we were), and for another, it was the loudest, stuffiest, sweatiest experience of my life. There were people making out all over the furniture, right there in plain view, but everyone was so drunk that no one cared. Even me. I couldn't process most of what I saw by the time I'd been there an hour because I was so full of beer, which I don't even like, that I couldn't walk in a straight line or put my cup down without spilling it. It's only now that I'm sitting here with Eleni in our own room, listening to a little Mediterranean guitar music, that I'm able to think it all through.

Since I'm being honest, I have to admit that this wasn't my first experience with alcohol. Some parents (*not* mine) would even serve it at volleyball parties because they figured it was safer than leaving the kids to go out looking for it elsewhere. But this was my first experience of Fraternity Row, and it was also my first experience of being so drunk I couldn't function. I'm an idiot to have done it for many obvious reasons, but I think the freakiest part for me is the feeling that I wasn't in control of myself the whole time I was drunk. I could have done almost anything, and there's no guarantee I would even know that I had.

I'm not going to make myself a nun or anything and renounce all parties for the rest of my life. But I don't think I'll go to another one with Pogo, and I have no plans at all to get drunk again. It will be a week before I can look at food with anything but revulsion.

It wasn't entertaining. I don't know who I met, I made myself sick, and no one I saw will recognize me and say hi this week because they don't remember me either. So what did I accomplish? I made it home safe. And that was definitely an accomplishment. In fact, it was an act of God, because I had nothing to do with it.

Wow. I'm remembering the days when I was too shy to even talk about boys with you, and now I've just told you I was so drunk I threw up. But on the other hand, I think I just admitted for the first time that God was working in my life.

I have to go to sleep. Tomorrow Eleni is taking me to her church. Yes, Saint Lydia, I'm finally going to church without planning to spend my entire time there staring at the floor. But please don't get your hopes up, because it will probably all come to nothing.

Love,

Lydia

Dear Lydia,

My hopes are raised more by the conclusions you have drawn about your drinking experience than by the fact that you are planning to attend church. I am delighted to learn you will be going to church, but I have always thought you would go eventually, so I am not surprised.

I agree that the most frightening aspect of drunkenness is the loss of yourself, the loss of control over your own actions and of your ability to think and to remember. It is as if you have counted yourself down to zero, or, to put it in your modern terms, as if you have turned on your car and then left the door open for any chance passerby to get in and drive it away.

It is indeed an act of God that you got home safely, because you could just as easily have been attacked, in your weakened condition, or have been run over by a car you did not see in time, or fallen prey to any number of other catastrophes. Your world is dangerous enough when you are fully in command of yourself.

You are precious to God, to me, to your family, and to your friends, and I beg of you not to risk yourself so carelessly again.

I believe that, in many cases, people seek intoxication or other mind-altering experiences because they do not have answers for the dilemmas in their lives. They cannot solve their problems, so they seek comfort in a pleasurable sensation that takes their mind away from their pain. But the pleasure is only temporary, because it does not solve the problem it is masking. Each time the pleasure fades, the pain returns, and the person is driven to take just one more drink, over and over again, to escape the pain. Without love and faith to build real solutions to pain that can be honestly confronted, many people stumble from one bad choice to the next, never solving the problem and often adding to it by their attempts to push it away. Although you must not enable a person seeking escape by means of alcohol or drugs, do not turn from such people without some feeling of pity, and in your heart, have mercy on their suffering. They do suffer terribly, you know, because the escape is never lasting, and the return is always to a reality that has worsened in their absence.

I wish you deep and restorative sleep, and I will look forward to seeing you in church tomorrow.

> *In Christ our Savior and our lasting escape,*
> *Saint Lydia*

33

December 5

Dear Saint Lydia,

Church was amazing.

We put on nice dresses and drove there in Eleni's car, which is so old and battered that she doesn't even lock it. She says the robbers are welcome to it if they think they can get it started.

Eleni is Greek, so she goes to a Greek Orthodox church, but she says there are lots of different kinds, even some that have the whole service in English and are mostly full of American converts (like the one my parents attend). The service we heard was about half in Greek and half in English, and the hymnal (or whatever you call it) had all the words in Greek on one side and all the words in English on the other side, so I was never lost.

It was so *foreign*. The music had a different sound, the air smelled of incense, there were bells, there were candles everywhere, and *beautiful* icons on every available inch of space. The church would have seemed crowded even without any people because there were so many icons. It seemed like the whole room was red and gold, and all the saints had deep dark eyes.

Everything was so *decorated*. The priest's robe was embroidered silk. People reached out their hands to touch it as he walked up to the altar during the service. The roof was a huge blue dome, and inside, right up in the top looking down at us, was the icon of Christ, watching us.

I have no idea who else was in church with us because I don't know any of them, and I was kind of surprised afterwards to realize I wasn't thinking about them anyway. You know how I am about church people. They give me a rash. But these ones didn't, probably because they weren't paying any attention to me and I wasn't paying any attention to them. They didn't show up this morning to bother me, and I didn't show up to bother them.

Eleni sang along with all the chanting, as she called it. Some people seemed to be singing along, and some people didn't. I saw a very tiny, very old lady wearing a lace veil and a black dress. She stood up most of the time, leaning on a shiny wooden cane, and she never said a word or made a sound. She turned once and smiled at me, so I smiled back.

They all stand up, did you know that? There were pews in the church (Eleni says lots of Orthodox churches don't even have pews), but we didn't sit in them except during the epistle reading and the homily, which was way shorter than a sermon in a Protestant church. I loved the sermon being short. I didn't come to hear someone's opinion about the Bible and how I should see it like they do. I just came to try out being in church, and everyone else there just came to worship. So they sing prayers all morning and then take communion, and then they go into the fellowship hall and eat and eat and talk and talk. Eleni did all the talking for us, and I wish I had been feeling like my usual self because, as I have said before, I love Greek food! It looked like a banquet to me, but Eleni said it's always like that, because they don't eat before church so they won't have anything else in their stomachs before they take the communion bread and wine, the body and blood of Christ.

The body and blood of Christ. It didn't seem as strange to think about that when I saw it all in context. I don't know why.

Love,

Lydia

P.S. Eleni bought me another icon at church. It's an icon of Mary and Baby Jesus, and he has his little arm around her neck. I never thought about it before, but he was her *baby*. She must have held him and nursed him and snuggled with him as he fell asleep. One day, if it seems right, I'll bring Trella an icon like this. It reminded me of her hand, always cradling her belly.

Dear Lydia,

That was me, dear girl. I was the very tiny, very old lady who smiled at you on your first day at church. I loved to see your face, especially your eyes gazing so intently around you, as deep and dark as the saints' eyes you searched out so carefully.

I must confess to giving Eleni a very slight nudge in the direction of the icon table. Her own loving knowledge of you did the rest. Your heart is full of thoughts of mothering, of your mother, of Trella, of your own eventual motherhood. It is good for you to be meditating under the eyes of the Mother of God.

With love and prayers,

Saint Lydia

December 25

Dear Saint Lydia,

Merry Christmas!

It's snowing again. It started snowing the night I got home from college, and it's been snowing at intervals ever since. I love snow! Tirsa and I bundled up and ran outside while it was still falling. We threw snowballs, slid down the hill in our backyard on cookie sheets, built a snow-person family, and ate snow in china bowls with maple syrup on it. Yum. The great gift of a much-younger sister is that you can fling yourself back into childhood sometimes to play with her. It makes her deliriously happy, and it makes me carefree for a while, forgetful of everything I know about life that she hasn't learned yet.

So much has happened since I came home a week ago that I haven't written to you yet. The day after I got home, Mom and Tirsa went to Aunt Aven's house for dinner and board games (this is a Saturday tradition they set up for Tirsa while I'm at school, and they keep it up even when I'm here on holidays). So Dad and I spent the afternoon and evening together.

We napped and read and watched the snow, and then we went for a walk, just as darkness fell. Our boots went crunch-hush-crunch-hush along the sidewalk drifts. The street lamps came on, and we walked from one patch of light to the next, crossing a blue snow lake on golden stepping stones. At the end of our street, there's a little row of shops, all decorated for Christmas with holly and tree lights. We went into a shop, and I found a baby Christmas dress in soft red velvet with white ribbon bows down the front like buttons, and it came with little bloomers and booties and a muffin-shaped red hat with a bow on top. Trella now knows she's having a girl, and the dress size said "9 months," which is about how old her baby will be next Christmas, so I bought it. Dad didn't say much, but he hunted around the shop and found a silver keepsake cup, a musical turtle, and a package of Trella-sized Christmas socks, and offered them as his gift. I hugged him for a full minute. We walked home arm-in-arm, and he built a fire in the fireplace for us while I wrapped the gifts in Christmas paper and packed them in a box to send to Trella.

The next morning, I put on snow boots and tramped out to the mailbox. The sun on the snow nearly blinded me. The entire world sparkled and glittered, and I could see flashes of blue and scarlet and gold in the ice crystals dripping from the trees. Our mailbox is red, and all it needed was a chickadee to perch on it with a spring of holly in his mouth to make the whole scene look like a Christmas postcard. I opened the mailbox, and right on top of the pile was a card for me. I didn't recognize the writing, but being curious, I opened it without waiting till I got back into the house.

It was from Paul! I have it here on the bed next to me as I'm writing to you. The front of the card is midnight blue with a single gold star near the top and gold lines radiating from it. Inside the card, in squarish handwriting, it says:

Lydia,

Merry Christmas and best wishes for the coming year.

Paul

I stood in the snow, staring at the card, trying to make it mean something that would tell me what made him send it. My dad said once that women are always reading more meaning into things than men have actually put there. But if Paul didn't mean something by it, why did he send it at all? We went to the same high school for four years before we went to the same college. This is my first Christmas card, or any card, from him. It must be some kind of return for the card I sent him with the fern spore case photos. Strange.

It's so neutral. The card could be seen as religious (the star could mean the star over the manger). Or not. The message is certainly pleasant, but it doesn't say much, does it? I wonder why he made a point of saying something (sending the card) that said almost nothing (one not-even-a-sentence inside).

Well, on to the next thing. So, tonight, Lauren, Jill, Tirsa, Tirsa's friend Rachel, and I had a Christmas cookie party. It was a riot! We made three kinds of cookies (Mom likes to make her Christmas activities Trinitarian): sugar cookies, spice cookies, and gingerbread cookies. When the cookies came out of the oven, we iced them, and we decided to make the gingerbread cookies into our friends. So we had a cookie for each of us, a Maria Louisa cookie, a Trella cookie (Jill made it look pregnant, which seemed kind of . . . tasteless?), and Lauren made a Paul cookie because Tirsa saw the card and announced to everyone that a "man from college" had sent me a card. *Grrreat.* So Lauren made the Paul cookie with nice brown hair, brown eyes, and pink and red hearts and kisses all over him. Lauren and Jill thought it was *so* funny. They made it run around the table and sweet-talk the me cookie in a squeaky voice. Okay, maybe it was a little funny. It certainly couldn't be anything else. The man hardly knows I'm alive.

And now night is falling, and I'm lying here watching the snowflakes drift down under the street lamp outside. I remember once, years ago, we went to a Christmas church service with my grandmother, who has since passed away. I was about six, and Tirsa hadn't been born yet. I wore my favorite blue velvet dress and "shiny shoes," and Mom put a blue ribbon in my hair. I remember feeling "dressed up" and proud of my pretties. I don't remember much about the service except that I sat next to Grandma, who smelled like cinnamon, and there were candles burning all around the church. They turned off the overhead lights for the service, and when the pastor read the part about the shepherds lying in the fields with their sheep, the choir began to sing in the back of the church. I thought it was the angels. I thought I could actually hear the Christmas angels singing in the night sky, above the candle stars.

Home feels warm and peaceful on this silent winter night.

Love and good wishes,

Lydia

Dear Lydia,

A blessing to you also in this celebration of the Savior's birth among us, and may you hear the angels rejoicing again as you did in childhood! In two thousand years of my own memories, I have never lost the sharp, bright joy I felt when I first learned how He came among us. Do you realize what it means? Do you realize that it is a defining act of love, the greatest love, flowing out to us from the mind of God? It is a comprehensive love, without pretense, extended to us because of our flaws, not in spite of them. I can never think of it without remembering the victory of Pascha, the trampling of death by death, made possible by this dear birth.

I loved reading about your walk through the snow with your father, and of his contributions to your Christmas gift to Trella and her baby. I suspect the most loveable aspect of his character is his gift for showing his love without many words. He is endeavoring to support both you and Trella, and you understand him clearly because of his simple sincerity and good will. God bless him.

I am delighted to hear that you received a Christmas card from Paul, and I must tell you that you cannot expect him to write volumes to you when you hardly exchange two words with one another in person. What encouragement have you given him, dear girl, that would lead him to believe you wished to hear from him? Intellectual self-confidence is no replacement for social self-confidence. The same intelligence that makes him so impatient with his fellow humans likely also tells him that they are not at ease in his company. I will pray that he learns how to mend this problem!

When you are old, not even as old as I am now, you will laugh over the Paul cookie whenever you remember it. You will not mind your present embarrassment. You will be too busy cherishing the innocence of these small trials and delights. Although it is sometimes difficult, it is a good gift to be young.

With prayers for you and for your family in this sacred season,
Saint Lydia

35

January 1

Dear Saint Lydia,

Happy New Year's Day! Today is my last day at home before I return to college. Mom and I haven't spent any time on our own during my vacation. Mostly, we stick with the family group and keep the conversation general and festive. This morning, I made waffles with Mom for a family breakfast, then we all played Go Fish and Hearts around the dining room table until lunch time. The mail came, and in it, I found a letter from Trella. I will copy out what she said so you can see it.

Dear Lydia,

This baby dress is my favorite Christmas gift. Not only from this year, but from my whole life. It is my first baby gift. I laid it out on my bed, and I could almost see my baby girl there in front of me, all dressed up for her first Christmas. Next year, I will give you a picture of her wearing it for Christmas.

I hope you can come to visit me again. We didn't say much, but the fact that you rode the bus all the way from college just to sit next to me means more than I can tell you. Please come again. Come when my baby is born, too. I will keep in touch with you, even if it's only by letter. I'm sorry I haven't been good at that for a while.

Love,
Trella

Reading this letter gives me a perfect feeling inside. The impulse to buy the baby dress came from love, and when I read this letter, I knew she felt my love even though I have never managed to tell her about it in words. I'm honored that she wants me to come when her baby is born. Our friendship is special now. It belongs only to us. It's not part of being on the volleyball team anymore, and that means it survived our lives going in separate ways. In fact, I'm better friends with her now than when we were on the team together. We aren't as good at talking to each other as Eleni and I are, but we seem to have a knack for understanding each other just the same.

It might be helpful if I had the same knack with Paul, but so far, he's a mystery. However, I decided to send him a Christmas card in return for his. Vacation's nearly over, so I sent it to his college address. I made the card out of a photo I took of the ice crystals sparkling in our tree by the mailbox. I thought about being as terse as he was, but that seemed a little childish, so I wrote what I would write to anyone.

Dear Paul,

Thank you for your good wishes! I hope you enjoyed your holiday as much as I enjoyed mine. We were out in the snow almost every day. I loved photographing the ice crystals at play in the sunlight.

Best wishes,

Lydia

I hope that doesn't sound strange. It seemed normal when I wrote it, but since mailing it, I've wondered at least ten times if it sounds corny, stilted, gushy, or like I'm making too much of the fact that he sent me a card. Probably he sent the same card to everyone he knows and it meant nothing. I hope Lauren and Jill don't tell the whole volleyball team about their lovey-dovey Cookie-Paul.

Good night, my friend.

Love,

Lydia

Dear Lydia,

You are a good friend, dear girl. You are supporting Trella's efforts at her own redemption, her wish to be a strong and loving mother for her baby daughter. Like your father, you have found a way to speak without words, and she has heard you and understood.

I doubt seriously that Paul sent the same card to everyone he knows, and I think your note to him is quite perfect. The right thing to do when talking to a friend is to be yourself. Your decision to speak naturally is the right decision. You are letting him see a side of yourself that you do not seem to share with your other friends. You are showing him your eyes on the world, your delight in the lovely intricacies of nature. God made these tiny miracles for us, and you

are safe in His presence when you gaze on them with such innocent attention.
Perhaps this little card-conversation of yours is a tiny miracle of its own.

In Christ who made glorious the lilies of the field,
Saint Lydia

36

January 20

Dear Saint Lydia,

I want to talk about a boy. His name is Jude, and he's tall with curly black hair, outrageous blue eyes, and subtle cologne. It's a new semester with new classes, and that's how we met—he's in my sociology class. He says his parents named him after the song "Hey Jude" by the Beatles (have you heard of them, I wonder?). He says he knows every song the Beatles ever recorded and will sing them all under my window if I'll invite him upstairs afterwards. I keep him at arm's length, just a little. He likes women who play hard to get.

I feel delicious. I feel sexy and intelligent and sparklingly witty because Jude laughs at almost every word I say. He turns everything into romance. Something as boring as the lunch menu can suddenly become a conversation about the mysteries of womanhood. Being with Jude is so simple. No guesswork. Just obvious admiration.

He's meeting me for lunch almost every day in the dining hall, and the third time he did it, Eleni said he's a charmer and I better watch myself. Then she asked me what classes I share with Paul (which just proves I should never have told her about the Cookie-Paul!). I think she's trying to distract me from Jude.

But it's too much fun! I don't want to be distracted from Jude. I'm not drinking, so I'm not being stupid. I'm just excited and happy and testing the waters to see if I can swim. This is so different from high school romance! There is nothing gauche about Jude.

Daydreaming,

Lydia

Dear Lydia,

Oh, my dear girl, be careful. Alcohol is not the only form of stupidity in which a young woman can indulge.

You have told me nothing that gives me confidence in this Jude. I know you would resent my saying so, but truly, look at what you have said. Is he a man of good character? Does he show kindness to you and to others? Laughter is a blessed gift, but only if it is the expression of other gifts.

If you have misjudged him (and what can you know of a man from mere flirtation!), you are risking a terrible awakening when his flaws and your indiscretion rise up to crush you.

Take care, dear girl. Testing the water is not a wise way to find out if you can swim. If you find that you cannot swim, you are still in the water, and you may drown.

In anxious prayer,

Saint Lydia

37

February 14

Dear Saint Lydia,

Remember Paul, the egomaniac? Guess what? He's arrogant and judgmental, too!

I think Jude is my boyfriend now, or he will be any minute, and today we were walking across campus on our way to class. He showed up outside our dorm to escort me to class, dressed like a pirate with a rose in his teeth and chocolate in both hands! I laughed and laughed, and every woman in sight was jealous of me. So maybe it was a little overdramatic for a Monday morning, but who doesn't want a little romance in her life on Valentine's Day?

So there we were, the pirate and the maiden, walking along and chatting flirtatiously, and I looked up and saw Paul coming toward us along the path. I was in a gorgeous mood, so I waved and smiled at him as he came up, and he gave me the nastiest look, shook his head, and walked right by without saying hello to either one of us. He couldn't have been ruder if he'd slapped me in the face! Jude said Paul was being rotten because he's jealous of Jude, but that's plain ridiculous, and it's not the feeling I got. I think he was *disapproving* of me. For what?! Jude and I weren't even holding hands, and it would have been none of his business if we had been. It would have been none of his business if we had been kissing passionately in the middle of the sidewalk!

It made me so angry. It spoiled my morning. Jude tried to joke me out of it. He said everyone knows that Paul is arrogant and boring. He even called him a party pooper in a ridiculous voice that was supposed to make me laugh. But I couldn't shake off my irritation. I hate being judged, and I hate it most when I'm given no chance to defend myself. Paul knows nothing about me and even less about my relationship with Jude.

I told Eleni when I got home, and she gave me her woman-of-the-world look and said, "Maybe it wasn't you he was judging. Maybe it was your choice of men!" I said, "What's that supposed to mean? I thought you liked Jude!" "I do," she said, "but I told you that boy is trouble, and maybe I'm not the only one who knows it."

There was no way I was going to answer that. I don't need to hear all about who on campus said what to whom about Jude, and believe me, Eleni would love to tell me. I don't want to fight with her. She's my friend. So I just don't let her talk to me about Jude.

I wish I could go running and work off my bad mood, but I have an English paper to write for tomorrow. Maybe I can find some themes of wrath and vindication in this wretched book.

Trying to focus on homework now,
Lydia

Dear Lydia,

Oh, how I wish you could hear me! Think what you are doing, dear girl. You have now told me that two people who know and care about you do not like Jude and are not pleased to see you with him. This is not a good sign.

Your anger at Paul seems tinged with guilt, and your decision not to let Eleni speak to you about Jude shows that you know she would have nothing good to say of him. This is not love, Lydia, and nor is it true romance. If you were in love with Jude truly, you would not respond to his courtship by considering how jealous other women are of his advances. Your friends would be sharing your joy, not meeting with your disapproval because they refuse to be blind to Jude's flaws.

Everything is wrong with this relationship. And what kind of relationship is it if he "turns everything into romance" without giving you any certainty that he is your "boyfriend"? How can you think he respects you when he makes you the object of such attention without offering you a sign that his intentions are honorable?

You may not believe that Paul knows you well enough to care about you, but the fact that he braved your likely anger to show you he thinks you are in danger demonstrates more caring than all the romantic foolery you will ever get from Jude.

I fear what will come of this adventure, dear girl. I will pray for your safe return to the protection of your friends.

In fervent prayer,

Saint Lydia

38

March 8

Dear Saint Lydia,

Are you there?

Are you there?

I know I haven't written to you for weeks, but something horrible has happened. It's horrible. Everything is horrible. No matter where I turn my head, everything smells like him, and it makes me want to throw up. Where is Eleni? Why doesn't she come home? I think I'm going to throw up.

I did. I threw up. I think I'm going to throw up again. I can't seem to stop. I can't stop crying either, and this paper's a mess because my hands are sweating and I'm crying. I said that already. I can't think at all, Saint Lydia. Why doesn't Eleni come home? Can't you make her come home? I have to throw up—

I'm sitting on the dirty laundry by Eleni's dresser because I can't stand up any more, but I'm all dirty so I can't sit on the bed, and the floor is cold and I'm cold already. Oh thank *God*. Eleni is back.

Here I am again. Eleni says I have to tell you exactly what happened, the whole thing. I don't even know if I can. I tried taking a shower. And then I took another shower, and I scrubbed the skin on my leg so hard that now there's a huge rash all over it. Or maybe I'm allergic to him and that's why there's a rash. I know I'm not making any sense. I'm so upset I feel like I'm going crazy.

I'm back. Eleni says to try again. So here I go. Oh please say you will still love me when I tell you, Saint Lydia.

It's Jude. I told you about him and then I disappeared from this journal because all I ever did when I wasn't in class was hang out with Jude and flirt with Jude and talk to Jude. I talked and talked. We must have talked for hours. I thought he wanted to know all this stuff about me because he was falling in love with me. I'm an idiot. How could I be such an idiot? Idiot, idiot, idiot. Eleni says to stop calling myself an idiot and tell you what happened.

It's a beautiful clear night outside, or it was, and Jude asked me to go for a walk down by the lake on west campus. We met at the gazebo, and when I got there, he was standing by the railing on the lake side. He didn't move at first, but he started to talk instead of joining me on the path, so I thought he must have changed his mind about walking and wanted to just hang out at the gazebo. It's a pretty place with a view of the lake and some gardens. It's sheltered, and no one can really see it from anywhere else, but it never entered my head to worry about that because I was with Jude.

He started sweet-talking like he always does, but something was different about his voice. Then he came toward me, and I thought he was going to kiss me, so I came toward him because I wanted to be kissed. But when his face got closer, I looked up and got a blast of sour beer breath and then I saw his expression. He was all flushed, and his eyes were bleary, and he looked hideous, like a wolf or some terrible predator, but I didn't react fast enough and he grabbed me. I was standing so close, waiting to be kissed by a man who loved me, and I couldn't back away quick enough, and then he was all over me, all over my mouth, all over my body, and he was sweaty like an animal, and I couldn't breathe. I couldn't draw in a breath. My lungs closed and his mouth was covering mine so I couldn't get to the air. I started clawing and kicking and struggling like I was drowning, drowning in a horrible sea of Jude, smelling like beer and sweat. I tried to do that knee move they taught us in high school gym class, but I couldn't breathe and I couldn't coordinate what my body was doing.

I don't even know how I escaped, Saint Lydia. I think maybe someone came down the path and Jude was afraid of getting caught. My memory is so confused, and I was gasping so hard for air as soon as he let go of me, and then I just started to run. I ran so fast and so hard that I ran into things, and I must have run all over campus before I got back here. And when I got into the room and turned on the light, I saw that one leg of my pants was soaking and slippery and sticky, and I knew what it was, and it made me so sick.

I feel the most horrible emptiness, worse than any pain I've ever felt in my life. I walked toward him expecting an expression of his love for me, and he showed me that he has no love for me at all. He wasn't making love to me, Saint Lydia. He was attacking me. He was hurting me for pleasure. I feel destroyed. I feel like he hates me and he made me think he loved me so that he could be sure that what he did tonight would hurt me as much as possible.

I feel like a shell. I feel like the whole universe is a black void, echoing with my screams.

Pray for me, Saint Lydia. Help me. Please help me. I don't know how I can live through this.

Lydia

Dear Lydia,

I will never stop loving you, even for a moment, and I pray for you even before you ask.

It is the absence of God, dear girl. That is what you have felt. That is the weapon with which your attacker has tried to batter you. He has taken his hatred and fashioned it into violence. Your goodness offended him, and he has made you suffer for it. This is from the devil. The terrible emptiness you feel is real. It is what evil makes for itself; it withdraws from God, and there is nothing to take His place. It is endless nothingness, a fate truly worse than physical death.

I know you can feel only pain tonight, but I will pray without ceasing that your senses will return to you. I will pray that you will be able to feel Eleni's love and protectiveness as she cares for you. I will pray that your feeling of security in the little home you have made together will return to you. I will pray that you will feel me hovering here, praying and watching, and wishing with all my heart that you could see me. I will pray that you will feel your own worth again, that you will know that you are a child of God, created deliberately in His image to fill a place in creation that could be filled by no one but you. I will pray especially that you will feel God, who is closest to you of all.

God has drawn as near to you as you will allow Him, Lydia. Your pain is keeping you from feeling His presence, as pain so often does, but He is there nonetheless, ready to make all right again as soon as you will let Him.

Hold tight to us, dear girl. Hold tight to your friends and let us lead you to God.

With grief and love,
Saint Lydia

39

March 9

Dear Saint Lydia,

Eleni and I just realized that I need to tell the RAs and call the police. Well, Eleni realized it, and she managed to talk me into it. It's really early in the morning, but she called them as soon as she had finished arguing me around to it. I'll write you more when it's over.

I'm back. An RA brought the policewoman up to our room in less than ten minutes. She helped me put all the clothes I had been wearing into a plastic bag (I took them off last night when I started showering every half hour), and then she took us all back to the police station with her. I had a long and rotten morning because they had to look all over me for bruises and things and photograph them all. The only reason I made it through was because Eleni kept popping in her head to tell me all the horrible vengeance she has planned for Jude and which of her bad-boy cousins is going to help her with each part of her dastardly plan. The people at the police station gave us coffee and bagels, and then we each had to give a statement. I had a picture of Jude that Eleni made me bring to give to the police, and they gave me a restraining order against Jude so he can't come near me again. The RA sent our names to the campus counseling office at the health center and said I have to go to a counselor, but fortunately, she let me go back to our room first. So we spent the rest of the afternoon in bed, eating chocolate and listening to loud Greek music to wash the whole experience out of our heads. It helped a little bit, but not very much.

Right after we got home from the police station, I called my mom and told her what happened. It was very hard to do it, but Eleni helped me. She helps me with every hard thing I have to do. She's like another mother. Eleni made the call and set me up by telling my mom basically what happened, and then she put me on the phone. My mom was very upset and told me that she was getting in her car right now to come to me.

And she did, Saint Lydia. She drove straight here. Two hundred miles without stopping and with nothing but her purse and her toothbrush. And when she got here, she just hugged me and hugged me for about an hour. She brought us dinner from somewhere, and then she and Eleni helped me collect up every single thing that came from Jude or made me think of him, all the silly little notes he wrote and stuff like that. Then my mom took us to some local picnic area with little charcoal grills, and we set fire to the whole collection. It was hugely satisfying. We burned every single thing that reminds me of him (except those wretched clothes I had to give to the police, but they still have them so I hope I never have to see them again, and if I do, I'll burn them, too). Then my mom called the registrar at home (where she got the number I have no idea, she says it's mama smarts and I will have them, too, one day), and she got me transferred to a different section of the sociology class where I met Jude so I won't see him in class either.

She had to go home tonight because she has to work tomorrow, but she and Eleni made some kind of pact before she left, so I guess she's delegated her mama-job to Eleni. It means so much to me that she came. She hardly even asked questions. She just got in her car and came. I've never felt so close to her. She left me her sweater to sleep with every night, and I have it wrapped around my pillow. I know it's silly, but I need something to hold onto.

Love,

Lydia

Dear Lydia,

God brings us gifts at the most surprising moments. This is the first time in any of your letters to me that you have told me that you could feel love from your mother. If this painful time bears no other fruit than that, you will have redeemed your sadness with this one treasure.

It is good to clear away every dirty scrap of that man's presence in your life. I applaud the bonfire! May the ashes blow harmlessly away into the earth and return only as grass and anthills and other things as innocent.

There is nothing silly about holding your mother's sweater every night. Why do you think we keep the icons in church? Why do we hold up the Gospel? Why do we savor our ancient rituals, century after century? There are many ways in which these things are valuable to us, on earth and in the spirit, but it is also true that human beings cling to what they love. When we love what is good and hold it tightly in our hands and press it against our hearts, our comfort in the beloved presence keeps us from falling away into evil. Hold fast to your talisman. Love is a guardian against all demons.

I will tell you a secret because I know you will not hear me until it is time. Eleni will be "another mother" to you. She will be your mother in Christ on the day of your baptism, and she will hold out her arms to you as you come up out of the water, with great joy in her heart. God bless her.

In Christ our merciful Lord,

Saint Lydia

March 10

Dear Saint Lydia,

I can't sleep. I haven't slept since it happened. I haven't gone to class or to the dining hall or anywhere. I just stay here and take showers all day long because I can't seem to get rid of the smell of him. I can't make my body feel clean. I keep trying and trying. I can't make myself go out the door because Jude is out there somewhere, and I don't know if I will know how to protect myself from him. I keep telling myself about the restraining order, but I can't make it sink in. I can't even answer the phone because I don't know what to say to anyone. I'm drowning.

Lydia

Dear Lydia,

You will not drown. God and your mother and Eleni and I will not let you. Do whatever comes next, even if it is something as simple as picking up

one foot and putting it down in front of the other to take a step. Do whatever you must to keep from giving up.

In constant prayer and holding you tightly,
Saint Lydia

41

March 12

Dear Saint Lydia,

I think it's a miracle. I will tell you what happened, and you can tell me if it's a miracle, and maybe I will hear your voice telling me.

On the third day after Jude attacked me, I was lying in bed with my eyes shut because I hadn't slept in three days and I was too tired to do anything else. I heard Eleni come in from dinner, and then I heard her talking in Greek on the phone. I figured she was talking to her mother, but no, she wasn't. The next minute, she dragged me out of the bed, put my shoes on my feet, and pulled the quilt off her bed. She took my hand as if I were a baby and walked me out of the room, down the stairs, out the door, and into her car. I just let her. I didn't have the energy to resist.

She drove me to church, opened the car door, took my hand, and walked me in, and there was Father Paul, the priest, and his wife. His wife said something to me, I don't know what, and she touched my face, very gently, and I wanted to respond, but I was all frozen up, so I just kept following Eleni's hand, pulling me along. We went into the sanctuary, right up to the icons in front of the altar, and stood in front of the icon of Christ. There was a candle burning in front of it. Father Paul and his wife came with us, and he and his wife chanted a prayer while he anointed us with holy oil. Eleni told me that's what it was. He made a cross on my forehead. I could feel the warm oil and his finger tracing the cross. Then he told Eleni they would be in his office if we needed them, and he and his wife went away.

Eleni wrapped us in her quilt and we sat on the rug in front of the icon of Christ. Eleni told me to look at Him and He would heal me. I was so tired it was hard to focus my eyes, so I just turned my face in the right direction. Sometimes I could see His face and sometimes I could only see the flame of the candle burning in front of Him. I put my head on Eleni's shoulder, and tears started raining down my face again.

But then I felt warm, and it wasn't from the quilt, Saint Lydia. The air around me felt warm, and the warmth seemed to soak into me like water. The little candle flame grew into a flood of light, brighter than daylight, golden and shining. Suddenly I smelled roses, thousands and thousands of roses, smelling the way roses smell in a garden late in the afternoon, when the sun has warmed them all day and the petals are soft and the scent is so sweet you can almost taste it.

Then I fell asleep.

I woke up on the floor of the church this morning with Eleni sitting beside me, waiting for me to wake up and sitting right where I would see her so I wouldn't be scared. But she wasn't the first person I saw when I woke up. When my eyes opened, the first thing I saw was the icon. I woke up with my face turned up to His face.

Father Paul and his wife stayed in the church all night so I could sleep there. Can you believe that? They hardly know me. It was a simple act of love that helped to save my life.

We came back to the dorm, and I showered (only once this time) and put on my clothes. I ate my breakfast and kept it down. I still feel shaky and unhappy, but I've come back from the dead, and I've discovered something on my way back.

The night Jude attacked me, I felt so empty. The whole world felt empty to me. It was like there was nothing good left anywhere; it was all a lie just like Jude was a lie. But last night, in front of the icon, I know there was a *Presence* there, Saint Lydia. I know it. It was like the opposite. Everything within me and around me was saturated with love, so full of love that it was soaked through and dripping everywhere.

I have put the pieces together, Saint Lydia. One was the absence of God, and the other was His presence. I still hurt all over, inside and out, but it's like when you turn your face away from something disgusting. You still know it's there, but it's not what you're looking at. What I am looking at is the fact that I want to go sit in front of the icon whenever I can. I want to be there in case He comes back.

Love,
Lydia

Dear Lydia,

My beloved girl, you are like the man possessed by demons after Christ freed him from his terrible captors. You are clothed and in your right mind and sitting at the feet of Jesus.

It was indeed His presence, Lydia. The Holy Spirit often brings a beautiful fragrance when He draws near to us, and God our truth and the source of all love brings light and warmth. You have had a small theophany of your very own, a blessing in the midst of your grief.

And look what the Holy Spirit has brought to you! You have put the pieces together, as you say. The hatred you felt from Jude was the absence of God, and the love you felt as you lay before the icon was His presence. It is as simple as that. When you know where to find God, everything else will fall into place.

The icon where you first found God will always be precious to you, but you must know that He will come to you in many places through your life. You do not need to stay there for fear of missing Him. Trust Him now that you have found Him. He is not limited to one time or place, and He is not so fragile that He will disappear if you do not stand perfectly still. Take your knowing of Him out into your life; you will find that He is quite portable. He will come with you wherever you go.

It is the third day, and you have risen up from the presence of death, just as Christ rose from the dead on the third day. Sin is death; when you have been in the presence of evil, you have come close to death even if your physical life did not appear to be in danger. But when you have been knowingly in the presence of God, you have come close to Life Itself. All the legions of hell cannot make the smallest mark on this vital Power.

Be comforted. You have found the only safety there is, and it is yours for the asking.

> In prayer and hope,
> Saint Lydia

42

March 14

Dear Saint Lydia,

Something happened today that I can't explain. Maybe you can.

Today I went back to classes for the first time since Jude attacked me. Eleni had an early class on the opposite side of campus, and she said she would do her best to get back here to walk with me so I wouldn't have to go alone.

I got dressed and got my books together, and then I started to feel a little panicky. I went to Eleni's dresser and touched all the icons and then rubbed my hands over my face, trying to bring something holy with me. My palms felt sweaty. I took a deep breath, locked the door behind me, and went downstairs, and there was Paul, waiting for me.

Paul.

I couldn't speak. I remembered his face when he saw me with Jude. I felt shamed and judged by that memory. I was sure he thought I was stupid for not seeing what he had seen about Jude. I couldn't look at him. I stood completely still.

Then he said, "Walk to class with me, Lydia," in a calm, friendly voice, and he took my hand and started walking. His hand was warm and dry. It reminded me of Eleni taking my hand and leading me off to church. So I went with him, one foot after the other. When we passed someone he knew, he said hi to them, and they said hi to us, and then we arrived at my class. Nothing had happened. I could breathe, and all the people we saw who knew us were so surprised to see Paul holding hands with a girl that they all stared at him instead of staring at me.

He found me a chair. I sat down, opened my bag, and got out a notebook and pen, and then it got easier. I just stared at the teacher and took notes and blocked everything else out. And when class was over, there was Paul, ready to walk me to my next class.

I don't think we said two words all day long. He just kept appearing, walking me to class, to lunch, back to class, and then back to my dorm. He waited till I got inside and started up the stairs, then he walked away.

I don't know why he came. Eleni says she didn't tell him to come. He came of his own accord.

He held my hand all day, Saint Lydia, and it didn't make me sick. I think he was offering me his protection. I don't understand, but I'm grateful.

Good night,
Lydia

Dear Lydia,

Hurrah! Here is Paul again, appearing in your life unsought. I am sure this is of the Holy Spirit, dear girl. What else could have brought him to your door at the moment of your need?

Whatever his manners may be in class, in the heat of academic debate, Paul's manners today are an example of unselfish courtesy and grace. If, as you say, no one has ever seen him holding hands with a girl, it must have cost him something to draw so much unwanted attention to himself. In a small way, he was laying down his life for you, Lydia, taking the embarrassment that would have been yours and bringing it down on himself instead.

I agree that he came to offer you his protection, and that is why his presence was comforting instead of sickening. Jude's actions were thoroughly selfish and destructive to the point of obscenity. Paul's actions today were wholly unselfish. Jude tried to consume you for his own pleasure. Paul is trying to support you for your good, even at his own expense. It is no wonder that his hand holding yours reminded you of Eleni's hand, holding you up and leading you away from your sorrow. Paul and Eleni are offering you their best efforts for your healing. You are blessed to have genuine friends beside you at the moment when you need them most.

When you are ready, let Paul see that you are grateful. If he knows that his effort succeeded, he will not mind the inevitable teasing from his friends.

  In Christ who takes all our pain upon Himself,
  Saint Lydia

March 15

Dear Saint Lydia,

Paul came again. He met me at the front door this morning and walked me everywhere I went today. I managed to look at him. He just smiled. Maybe he's not judging me after all. You don't take so much trouble for someone you've decided is a hopeless idiot.

I still try not to make eye contact with anyone else. It feels like everyone on campus knows what happened to me, and I don't want to talk about it with any of them. I'm sure they're talking about me behind my back, but at least I don't have to hear them.

My professors are giving me extra time to complete assignments that I missed. It's very nice of them, but it's hard to talk to them about it. I try to keep the conversations as short as possible, and most of them don't force the issue.

Eleni just got home. She's going to teach me how to play chess tonight. How does she know how to play chess? Where did she get this little chess set she's getting out? One of her cousins, probably. I'm sure she will tell me. She keeps finding things for me to do, to keep my mind focused on something harmless. She laughs and tells me idle hands are the devil's playthings.

Eleni makes me smile.

Love,

Lydia

Dear Lydia,

Your instinct is correct. No matter what anger and fear he felt on the day he saw you with Jude, Paul is not judging you. He is serving you. I find his actions remarkably Christian. I am certain his feelings for you are his primary motivation, but the fact that these feelings find expression in such wise and gentle ways gives me hope for his future. And perhaps for yours also, in God's time!

Learning to look up again and to meet the eyes of people around you will take time. You fear what you will see in their eyes, and you fear the necessity of talking to people who catch your eye to initiate a conversation. Your wound is still too raw. You can hardly bear to look at it yourself, so you resist the idle curiosity and morbid interest you may sense around you.

Be thankful for Eleni, with whom you can share the whole burden of your troubles, and for Paul, who came to you without a single word of explanation. Keep talking to Eleni and walking with Paul so that you do not lose the habit of connection with those who care for you. As for the rest, time blows away one scandal with another, and in a few weeks, everyone will have forgotten you and fixed their greedy gaze on someone else. Until we come again into the pristine charity in which God created us, time passing is sometimes the best solution here on this fallen earth.

Grace to you, and peace,

Saint Lydia

March 26

Dear Saint Lydia,

I'm back to normal life, more or less. Maria Louisa hugs me whenever she sees me and says the hug is from Trella too, who knows what happened because Maria Louisa told her for me. Lauren and Jill seem uncomfortable around me, like they don't know what to say, and I just don't have it in me to make things easier for them. Everybody else has stopped asking me questions because Eleni tells them to shut up or she will get her cousins to kill them and make it look like an accident. My parents filed a lawsuit against Jude, who has disappeared (according to Eleni's friend whose boyfriend knows Jude). He must have gone home or something. I'm trying not to think about him or the lawsuit or much of anything at all, but I'm managing to get up and go through my days pretty well.

Paul comes every morning to walk me through my day. He doesn't hold my hand anymore, but we talk now.

Mom and Eleni got me little rose-scented sachets and rose-scented soap and lotion, so I can smell roses around me every day. It's my personal garden, invisible but strongly present. It keeps the memory of my night by the icon fresh and tangible, and it's a good antidote to memories of Jude. When I have nightmares, I tuck a sachet into my pillowcase and fall asleep again in peace.

I'm also taking a women's self-defense course (and yes, of course, Eleni's taking it with me) to help me overcome the awful feeling of powerlessness I had on that night, and to prepare me to defend myself if there's ever a next time. Personally, the idea of getting close to any man for any reason ever again *disgusts* me, but my counselor says this feeling will pass with time. I wish time moved more quickly. I miss feeling good. I miss normal, uneventful moments of contentment.

In the meantime, I joined a catechumen class that Father Paul is giving at Eleni's church. Everything suddenly got very simple for me. I just want to be close to the Presence I felt that night at the icon, and the Orthodox Church is where He is.

At first, I wanted to rush right over to church and fling myself into the baptism water, but Eleni told me that if I did that, I would just react against it and end up thinking that I'd done it only because I was so upset and trying to protect myself. She said to do it the right way and in the right time so that I don't set myself up to doubt my faith just as I'm starting to have any. Father Paul agreed with her, so I'm taking the class, and for the moment, I'm content with that. It's nice to have somewhere to go that's completely separate from school. Going into the church for class is like going into another world, and what a relief that is, given how tough my usual world is right now.

Off to get some homework done so I don't get too far behind in my classes.

Love,

Lydia

Dear Lydia,

There is nothing so beautiful to me about Orthodox Christianity as the many ways in which I can see how it is a faith in God's image. Orthodoxy comes naturally to human beings because they are created in His image, too, and the practices and teachings of the Church are so clearly the things a human being does naturally to express faith and reverence and worship.

An Orthodox church is heaven on earth. It is a little piece of the kingdom, and each time you come there, you are walking out of the world and into heaven. You are coming close to Christ as His Holy Spirit descends on the bread and wine. You are worshipping with all the saints, visible and invisible to you.

And what have you just told me? That going into the church is like going into another world! You have said this simply because it is how you feel. But it is how you feel because you are created in God's image, and you feel the pull of that image when you enter the greater image, His church.

Eleni is wise to advise you not to "rush right over to church and fling yourself into the baptism water." Remember how you worried that you would doubt your faith if you thought you converted under pressure from your parents? How much more would you doubt it if you thought you converted under pressure from your own personal trauma? How often would you second-guess it and undermine it as you found psychological analyses to explain away all that you felt?

You have come so far. Walk along the whole path, all the way to the end. Then you will be contented. You will be satisfied that you have finished this stage of the journey, and your mind will be free for whatever adventures await you on the other side of this door you are entering through baptism.

Have patience also with your lacerated heart. You will always feel disgust in the presence of men like Jude, and this is right and healthy. It is a protection to you and all that you hold sacred. But in time, the wounds will heal and there will be room in your heart again for other, happier emotions. Love is your life, dear girl. You were made to love and to be loved, and this one act of violence cannot change your nature if you choose that it shall not.

May the grace of God envelop you and give you peace.

In Christ our Savior,

Saint Lydia

March 29

Dear Saint Lydia,

I had a conference call today with my parents and our lawyer. The lawsuit went to mediation because our lawyer says Jude's lawyer is right that if we go to court, it will go nowhere. There was no one there when Jude attacked me except Jude and me, so it's his word against mine. I never actually said "No" or "Stop" because I couldn't get my mouth free to do it, but his lawyer can make that look like Jude didn't know I wanted him to stop.

So Jude will probably get off with what my dad calls "a slap on the hand." I can keep the restraining order, so he won't come anywhere near me again, but what about the next girl? Was I just a fluke? Why do I think he didn't learn anything from this and will pull the same nasty trick on someone else as soon as the attention is off him?

It makes me sick. There's nothing I can do about it, but it makes me feel like what happened to me is now okay with everyone. I don't mean with my family and friends, but it's like the legal system is saying that it wasn't that big a deal, that somehow I should have handled it better or that I blew it out of proportion. It hurt me so badly that to hear it belittled like this makes me feel worthless.

I gave up. I said I wanted the restraining order and that I was going back to class. I want this lawsuit to be over as quickly as possible. My parents can't afford big-time lawyers to turn this into a made-for-TV movie plot where I take on the system, have a huge courtroom drama, and beat Jude to a pulp in front of the whole American public. I had to cut it short. It was time to go.

I wish I could comfort myself with the thought that at least Jude won't ever be able to get a date if he comes back to college here again. The story got around—you know how it is with scandal, it spreads faster than melted butter. But the thing is, there are always those girls who just don't believe it, not about someone smart and sexy like Jude. You can tell them the guy's a jerk, but they think he won't be a jerk to them. They think everyone else just didn't understand him, that he's never experienced real love like he will with them and that will make it all different, or they think it's going to be fun to be in love with a "bad boy." *Ugh.* Remember my totally naïve conversation with you about "bad boys"? Jude *is* a bad boy. He's actually bad. And there was nothing romantic or fun about it at all.

Sigh. It's okay. I'm going to my catechumen class in fifteen minutes, and then Eleni and I are going out for ice cream as far away from campus as we can get and still be able to drive back in time for bed.

Love,
Lydia

Dear Lydia,

On earth, there is not always justice, dear girl. What Jude did to you is inexcusable. He should be punished for it, and he should be kept from doing the same wrong to other women. But as you have seen, these things may not happen. What happens on earth is so often not what should happen. Consider the martyrs of the early Church. Surely there was nothing fair or just in their deaths. They were killed over a religious disagreement and to satisfy the insatiable lust for power.

But you must also consider in how many cases the martyrs brought their deaths upon themselves by professing their Christian faith. If they had not declared themselves to be Christians, many of them could have escaped martyrdom. So why did they do it?

They did it because although they were fully aware that there would be no justice for them on earth, they were just as fully aware that they would meet with Justice Itself after death. They were so confident in the happiness awaiting them that they were able to face the pain that stood between them and their ultimate blessing.

You are not asked, in most parts of the modern world, to suffer martyrdom for your faith. But you are still asked to face wrongdoing, injustice, cruelty, malice, and all the oppressive acts of the wicked. You will destroy yourself with raging against them. You must fight them whenever you can, but you must never forget that in the face of the final reality, they are not important. Injustice on earth can never impair the ultimate justice of Christ's love, of His victory over death, and of the joy and peace coming to us in His kingdom after death.

In confidence and anticipation,
Saint Lydia

46

April 10

Dear Saint Lydia,

Trella's baby girl was born at sunrise, 7 pounds, 7 ounces, 21 inches long, black eyes, black wispy curls, tiny fingers and toes. Trella called me at 7:30, an hour after the baby was born. She named her Amara Grace. Amara means "beloved."

Paul drove me to the hospital to see Trella and Amara. No Greyhound bus ride this time. I don't seem to go anywhere without him these days. Maria Louisa and Lauren came with us, and we crowded into Trella's room with balloons, a baby workout suit in our old team colors, and a volleyball we all signed. I brought a gift of my own, too, a tiny icon of Mary and her Baby, painted on a pendant that can be pinned inside Amara's bassinet.

I held Amara, Saint Lydia. I climbed into Trella's hospital bed and we sat together, watching Amara sleep in our arms. Trella gave me half of the pillow, and I leaned back and held Amara against my chest. I could feel her small weight, the warmth of her melting into me. I could feel the shape of my body matching the shape of hers, as if we were two interlocking pieces of a puzzle that were made together. "Smell her," whispered Trella, and I breathed in her baby scent and her downy hair brushed my lips.

Trella is clean and golden today. Light glows out of her. There is nothing left in the world for her but Amara. She has run the first lap of her race, and won.

Hours later, I can still feel Amara in my arms. I keep hugging myself, to savor the feeling, and it strikes me that Amara and I have something in common. Although she doesn't know it, bad things have happened to Amara. Her father has already abandoned her, her mother has struggled from the moment of her conception, and her family is divided with frustration and regret. But Amara is new and perfect and sweet. She isn't connected with any of this grief. She is wrapped in Trella's love. She is the perfect fruit that blossomed on the imperfect tree.

I don't have Amara's innocence, but in my own way, I am newborn, and my birth came to me from the hardest, saddest days of my life. Perhaps it is the nature of birth. Labor hurts, but it brings new life. Perhaps we only achieve beauty after pain.

> Love,
> Lydia

Dear Lydia,

Beloved girl, it seems that some of our words are able to cross the boundary between us, or perhaps it is only that our closeness to one another turns our inward eyes in the same direction. Months ago, I told you that pain exists because of beauty and beauty exists because of pain, and now you have given my words back to me, out of your own knowledge. Trella's great pain has brought her the deepest love of her life, just as your own suffering has led you to your spiritual birth. Love has brought you to life, just as Trella's love has brought Amara.

Labor pains, physical and spiritual, are the mark of the fallen world that militates against any new creation. Yet they are also an imprint of the Paschal victory, the sign of the Triumphant Creator who uses death to defeat death. The pain that seeks to crush out all new life is turned against itself by God, who lets the struggle sharpen our senses to more fully experience the victory. The light you saw glowing in Trella today was the surge of exaltation rising within her when Amara came into her arms at dawn.

A blessed peace and joy from our victorious Lord be upon you all,
Saint Lydia

47

April 16

Dear Saint Lydia,

I went for a walk with Paul. Not a walk to class. Just a walk.

He found me in the library behind a pile of reference books. I was staring at my laptop, watching the cursor blink and mumbling possible thesis statements to myself. He stood there watching me until I noticed him, then he said, "Is that important? The sun is shining. Come for a walk with me." I said I would come only if he could help me write a thesis statement comparing the classical mindset to the romantic mindset as expressed in French literature of the eighteenth century. Of course he could. He could probably write classical literature on the spot, too. Even romantic literature.

I don't mean "romantic" in the sense of romance. It's a literary term. I'm not asking anyone for any romance, literary or otherwise.

Although it *is* a curious thought, the idea of Paul writing romantic literature of the romantic kind. What is a brilliant, impatient, oddly understanding man like when he's in love? Who does he fall in love with, I wonder?

We went for a walk. We left my laptop in his car and wandered off campus, down one little residential street after another, for two hours, talking all the way. I want to tell you what we said.

It began with Trella's baby. He drove me to see Amara, remember, so he asked how she and Trella are getting along now that they're at home. I told him, and then I started talking and I couldn't stop. I didn't realize how much I wanted to explain to him, how much I wanted him to know that I had seen his scorn, that I believed in Jude until he betrayed my belief, that I felt so close to Amara's baby because I'm trying to be like her, a new life, a recovered innocence. I even told him about the night by the icon and about the transforming realization that I had escaped my own doubts long enough to find God.

When I ran out of words, we were all the way across town, walking under the cherry blossoms along the riverbank. We stood still in my silence. The waning light flickered over the water like a thousand candle flames. His face had an alert expression, as if for some memory suddenly returning. "You just needed a more powerful lens," he said, and he smiled, looking down into my upturned face like an old friend.

In contemplation,
Lydia

Dear Lydia,

If you wish to know what Paul will be like when he falls in love, turn and look at him. Paul is in love, and he is in love with you.

Dear girl, this boy is giving you lessons in romance of a kind that Jude and his like will never achieve. There is no greater romance than to be known well and still loved, with a compassion that does not require pretense. Paul tried to warn you when you were in danger. He offered you his protection and undemanding companionship when you were in need. He listened to your story with an understanding heart, and his reply shows that he has taken time to know who you are, to remember what memories you hold in common and to perceive what meaning attaches to them. Perhaps most precious is his sincere belief in your moment of transformation. The man who can truly see and confirm the changes you make in your spiritual self is a gift from God.

It seems you do not yet know what Paul's faith may be. I remain convinced that he came into your life on the breath of the Holy Spirit. Eternal love demands eternal faith, and time must pass before you will know whether you share these two gifts with Paul. For now, he is your good friend, and his love gives you strength to do good work. What is good comes from God and can be trusted.

> Content to await the unveiling of this mystery,
> Saint Lydia

May 12

Dear Saint Lydia,

My catechumen classes are coming to an end, and it's almost time for me to be baptized. Usually, they ask you to participate in classes for almost a year, but Father Paul has helped me study in a shorter time because, as he says, he wants me to "rejoin" my family soon.

Today, I asked Eleni to be my godmother, and she said yes. She burst into tears, wrapped her arms around me, and rocked me back and forth, singing the baptism hymn. It's a verse from Galatians, set to chant music, and it goes like this:

"As many of you as have been baptized into Christ have clothed yourselves in Christ. Alleluia!"

Eleni said we will walk around the baptismal tub three times, chanting this hymn and carrying candles, at the completion of the sacrament. For a few minutes, she gave me an enthusiastic description of the elements of the service and started a list of what she will need to bring (white towels, a white dress for me to wear at the end of the service, a baptismal candle to decorate, a cross on a chain for the priest to bless and place around my neck), but then she tossed the pencil and paper in the air, turned on her joyful Greek music full blast, and went dancing down the hall, singing at the top of her lungs. And so her godmotherhood has begun!

And now, I want to ask you to be my name saint. I have your name already, but this has never had anything to do with you. It was my grandmother's name. Now, I want it to be your name that I'm taking on as a new name, in my baptism.

I have a very strong feeling that you like this idea. I think you are saying yes.

Thank you, my good friend. I love you.

    Yours,

    Lydia

Most Dear Lydia,

Yes! I am saying yes! I am overjoyed to be your name saint and to know that you have felt my joy yourself.

Your name will be like yourself. When you are baptized, you will come up from the water looking just as you have always looked, on the outside. To other people, you will appear the same. But you will be a new creation, a new woman rising up from her birth into new life. And so it will be with your name. It will appear as the same name you have had from your natural birth, but you will know that in truth it is a new name, newly given and received.

It is a change of heart, dear Lydia, a change from the inside that will one day shine out of you like rays of brilliant light.

    In great delight and faith now justified,

    Saint Lydia

May 14

Dear Saint Lydia,

Here's a moment I want to share with you, my best of friends. I invited five people to come to my baptism, and three said yes. Their answers suddenly seemed like a map of my year, like a red line connecting the dots to show where I started, where I journeyed, and where I stand now.

I invited Trella, Maria Louisa, Lauren, Jill, and Paul. I called the girls on the phone this afternoon, one right after another. Trella is eager to come because she wants to be there for me like I was there for her. Besides, she wants to baptize her baby in a church, so she thinks this will be a good learning experience. Maria Louisa said yes enthusiastically because she's Super-Catholic and Orthodoxy is close enough, at least in her mind. Lauren said something vague and supportive like she always does, but she can't make it because she has a prior commitment. Jill's response was plain weird. She started out joking about it, and when I didn't respond to her humor, she got uncomfortable and offered this jumbled explanation about how she's in a Buddhist phase in her spiritual path right now and isn't attending Christian ceremonies. She must have figured out that you can't be Catholic and Buddhist at the same time . . . but I wonder what a Buddhist phase is and what she will be next.

I invited Paul in person. I took one of my fern photos and wrote on the back, "Dear Paul, I am celebrating my discovery of the more powerful lens, and I want you to be there. Will you come to my baptism into the Orthodox Christian Church? Love, Lydia." I gave it to him when he walked me home after dinner tonight. He grinned when he saw the photo, then turned it over to read the note at my request. I felt nervous suddenly, wondering how he would respond. I looked up into his face, waiting for a sign.

He put the card into his pocket and cleared his throat a few times. He looked away across the quadrangle, then back at me, and suddenly he took a quick step and gathered me into his arms. I could hear his heart beating in his chest. I leaned against him and let him hold me close. I felt warm and safe. There was no need for words. I know he will come.

I'm sleepy, Saint Lydia. I remember that I've known sadness, but it's far away from me tonight. My best friends are near to me: Eleni, my confidante, Trella, my fellow traveler, and Paul, my unexpected strength.

Eleni's music is playing, our icons are glowing in the lamplight, and the room smells like roses. I have found the end of my journey in the beginning of another journey. I am content.

In love and peace,

Lydia

Dear Lydia,

My dear friend, your letter fills my heart. To see you recovering your sense of love and goodness, to know that your trials have not broken you, and to find that this blessed boy has shown you his heart are precious gifts to me.

Your three friends, Eleni, Trella, and Paul, are the fruits of your journey. You yourself are a better friend now to them, as they are to you. Love is reciprocal, an upward spiral of shared gifts and of life that renews itself, over and over, leading us into the presence of God.

Your first journey has ended, and you will know hard days on the new journey you are beginning, but for now, I pray you will savor this moment of grace. God has granted your wish. You will no longer journey alone. And now, you have invited Paul to your baptism. Who knows what fruit may ripen from that seed?

> With thanks to the Holy Spirit, the Lord, the Giver of Life,
> Saint Lydia

50

May 15

Dear Saint Lydia,

Today, I called my mom and told her I'm going to be baptized. I talked to Dad and Tirsa too, but I want to tell you most about my conversation with my mom.

All three of them are very happy and excited, and they're going to take time off from work and school to drive here for my baptism. I didn't tell them until now because I thought it would be hard to do, but it wasn't. So much has happened in my life since the days when I was overanalyzing their conversion that I just can't feel the same way about it. I know why I'm converting, so I know it wasn't because of pressure from them. They weren't even there when it happened. So I'm happy to have them present when I'm baptized. It will be an important day in my life, and I want the people I love to be there.

Tirsa took the news calmly and said, in her wise little owl voice, that she knew I would do it eventually and she wants to hear Eleni talking in Greek. My dad kept saying, "Are you sure, baby? I want you to be happy, but are you sure?" I told him I was sure, and he said, "Well, in that case, I can't wait to be there."

I talked to my mom the longest. I could hear her taking the phone out on the porch, like she always does when she wants to have a private conversation, but this time, it was a private conversation with me. I felt like I had crossed some invisible barrier, like now I'm part of a different world, the adult world I used to look into from the outside.

She told me how happy she is with my decision, and then she told me that getting baptized as an adult is like having a heart transplant. She said when they put in a new heart, the surgeon has to cut all the blood vessels away from the damaged heart and then reattach them to the new heart. She said the same thing happens when you are baptized. The broken heart is taken out of you, and you have to reattach all the strands of your inner life to this new heart you have taken in. Every time you want to make a decision, there is your new faith waiting for you. Your choices, your habits, your responses to things, your feelings (much more than you expect them to) all have to be reattached to this new heart.

She said that after she was baptized, all the parts of her spiritual life that had been neglected or unexplored started to *hurt*. They suddenly came to life and were stiff and sore from lack of use. Old problems she hadn't dealt with came back up inside her, old feelings, old thoughts. It was like they had been waiting, or lying dormant, but now that she had turned on the light, so to speak, she had to deal with all the things she had put aside or closed her eyes on before.

I asked her if being baptized had made things worse for her, because it sounded like it had made her unhappy. She said she had a hard time for a little while after her baptism, and she reminded me how much she and I had struggled with each other through the summer. But then she regained her balance, and things began to get better and better. She said she could feel life inside herself where there had been no life before, and she couldn't get enough of it. Her love for Orthodoxy just grew and grew, even in ways she hadn't expected. She said her advice is to be prepared for the hard time, but to just live through it in the knowledge that it will pass, and that the faith that inspired me to be baptized will turn into love. She said, "I go to church because I love it."

I said, "I love you, Mom." And she said, "I love you, Lydia." And it was enough. She can finally speak, and I can finally hear.

I am a little seed, planted in the earth, and my roots are reaching for the water, and my stem is climbing to the air. I am coming to life. I will leave my tight, dark casing and burst into wide green leaves and bright red flowers in the light.

Always yours,
Lydia

Dear Lydia,

Your mother has spoken the words for me. I will give praise to God for your new heart and for the renewal of love and peace between you and your mother.

In Christ our blessed and complete delight,
Saint Lydia